D1080218

The Small Hand

The Small Hand

A Ghost Story

SUSAN HILL

P

PROFILE BOOKS

First published in Great Britain in 2010 by
PROFILE BOOKS LTD
3A Exmouth House
Pine Street
London ECIR OJH
www.profilebooks.com

3 5 7 9 10 8 6 4

Printed and bound in Great Britain by
Clays, Bungay, Suffolk

A CIP catalogue record for this book is available from the British Library.

ISBN 978 1 84668 236 0
eISBN 978 1 84765 317 8

The paper this book is printed on is certified by the © 1996 Forest
Stewardship Council A.C. (FSC). It is ancient-forest friendly. The printer
holds FSC chain of custody SGS-COC-2061

FSC
Mixed Sources
Product group from well-managed
forests and other controlled sources
Cert no. SGS-COC-2061
www.fsc.org
© 1996 Forest Stewardship Council

To Robert, cher ami pour beaucoup d'années,
for so many things
Et aussi pour sa Claudine

The Small Hand

One

It was a little before nine o'clock, the sun was setting into a bank of smoky violet cloud and I had lost my way. I reversed the car in a gateway and drove back half a mile to the fingerpost.

I had spent the past twenty-four hours with a client near the coast and was returning to London, but it had clearly been foolish to leave the main route and head across country.

The road had cut through the Downs, pale mounds on either side, and then run into a straight, tree-lined stretch to the crossroads. The fingerpost markings were faded and there were no recent signs. So that when the right turning came I almost shot past it, for there was no sign at all here, just a lane

1

and high banks in which the roots of trees were set deep as ancient teeth. But I thought that this would eventually lead me back to the A road.

The lane narrowed. The sun was behind me, flaring into the rear-view mirror. Then came a sharp bend, the lane turned into a single track and the view ahead was dark beneath overhanging branches.

I slowed. This could not possibly be a way.

Was there a house? Could I find someone to put me on the right road?

I got out. Opposite me was an old sign, almost greened over. THE WHITE HOUSE. Below, someone had tacked up a piece of board. It hung loose but I could just make out the words GARDEN CLOSED in roughly painted lettering.

Well, a house was a house. There would be people. I drove slowly on down the track. The banks were even steeper, the tree trunks vast and elephantine.

Then, at the end of the lane I came out of the trees and into a wide clearing and saw that it was still light after all, the sky a pale enamelled silver-blue. There was no through road. Ahead were a wooden gate and a high hedge wound about with briars and brambles.

All I could hear were birds settling down, a thrush singing high up on the branches of a walnut tree and blackbirds pinking as they scurried in the under-growth. I got out of the car and, as I stood there, the birdsong gradually subsided and then there was an extraordinary hush, a strange quietness into which I felt I had broken as some unwelcome intruder.

I ought to have turned back then. I ought to have retraced my way to the fingerpost and tried again to find the main road. But I did not. I was drawn on, through the gate between the overgrown bushes.

I walked cautiously and for some reason tried not to make a noise as I pushed aside low branches and strands of bramble. The gate was stuck halfway, dropped on its hinges, so that I could not push it open further and had to ease myself through the gap.

More undergrowth, rhododendron bushes, briar hedge growing through beech. The path was mossed over and grassy but I felt stones here and there beneath my feet.

After a hundred yards or so I came to a dilapidated hut which looked like the remains of an old ticket booth. The shutter was down. The roof had rotted. A rabbit, its scut bright white in the dimness of the bushes, scrabbled out of sight.

I went on. The path broadened out and swung to the right. And there was the house.

It was a solid Edwardian house, long and with a

wide verandah. A flight of shallow steps led up to the front door. I was standing on what must once have been a large and well-kept forecourt – there were still some patches of gravel between the weeds and grass. To the right of the house was an archway, half obscured by rose briars, in which was set a wrought-iron gate. I glanced round. The car ticked slightly as the engine cooled.

I should have gone back then. I needed to be in London and I had already lost my way. Clearly the house was deserted and possibly derelict. I would not find anyone here to give me directions.

I went up to the gate in the arch and peered through. I could see nothing but a jungle of more shrubs and bushes, overarching trees, and the line of another path disappearing away into the darkening greenery.

I touched the cold iron latch. It lifted. I pushed. The gate was stuck fast. I put my shoulder to it and it gave a little and rust flaked away at the hinges. I pushed harder and slowly the gate moved, scraping on the ground, opening, opening. I stepped through it and I was inside. Inside a large, overgrown, empty, abandoned garden. To one side, steps led to a terrace and the house.

It was a place which had been left to the air and

the weather, the wind, the sun, the rabbits and the birds, left to fall gently, sadly into decay, for stones to crack and paths to be obscured and then to disappear, for windowpanes to let in the rain and birds to nest in the roof. Gradually, it would sink in on itself and then into the earth. How old was this house? A hundred years? In another hundred there would be nothing left of it.

I turned. I could barely see ahead now. Whatever the garden, now 'closed', had been, nature had taken it back, covered it with blankets of ivy and trailing strands of creeper, thickened it over with weed, sucked the light and the air out of it so that only the toughest plants could grow and in growing invade and occupy.

I should go back.

But I wanted to know more. I wanted to see more. I wanted for some reason I did not understand to come here in the full light of day, to see everything, uncover what was concealed, reveal what had been hidden. Find out why.

I might not have returned. Most probably, by the time I had made my way back to the main road, as of course I would, and reached London and my comfortable flat, the White House and what I had found there in the dusk of that late evening would have receded to the back of my mind and before long been quite forgotten. Even if I had come this way I might well never have found it again.

And then, as I stood in the gathering stillness and soft spring dusk, something happened. I do not much care whether or not I am believed. That does not matter. I know. That is all. I know, as surely as I know that yesterday morning it rained onto the windowsill of my bedroom after I had left a window slightly open. I know as well as I know that I had a root canal filling in a tooth last Thursday and felt great pain from it when I woke in the night. I know that it happened as well as I know that I had black coffee at breakfast.

I know because if I close my eyes now I feel it happening again, the memory of it is vivid and it is a physical memory. My body feels it, this is not only something in my mind.

I stood in the dim, green-lit clearing and above my head a silver paring of moon cradled the evening star. The birds had fallen silent. There was not the slightest stirring of the air.

And as I stood I felt a small hand creep into my right one, as if a child had come up beside me in the dimness and taken hold of it. It felt cool and its fingers curled themselves trustingly into my palm and rested there, and the small thumb and forefinger tucked my own thumb between them. As a reflex, I bent it over and we stood for a time which was out of time, my own man's hand and the very small hand held as closely together as the hand of a father and his child. But I am not a father and the small child was invisible.

Two

It was after midnight when I got back to London and I was tired, but because what had happened to me was still so clear I did not go to bed until I had got out a couple of maps and tried to trace the road I had taken in error and the lane leading to the deserted house and garden. But nothing was obvious and my maps were not detailed enough. I needed several large-scale Ordnance Survey ones to have any hope of pinpointing an individual house.

I woke just before dawn and as I surfaced from a dreamless sleep I remembered the sensation of the small hand taking hold of my own. But it was a memory. The hand was not there as it had been there, I was now quite sure, in the dusk of that strange garden. There was all the difference in the world, as there was each time I dreamed of it, which I did often during the course of the next few weeks.

I am a dealer in antiquarian books and manuscripts. In the main I look for individual volumes on behalf of clients, at auction and in private sales as well as from other bookmen, though from time to time I also buy speculatively, usually with someone in mind. I do not have shop premises, I work from home. I rarely keep items for very long and I do not have a large store of books for sale at any one time because I deal at the upper end of the market, in volumes worth many thousands of pounds. I do collect books, much more modestly and in a disorganised sort of way, for my own interest and pleasure. My Chelsea flat is filled with them. My resolution every New Year is to halve the number of books I have and every year I fail to keep it. For every dozen I sell or give away, I buy twenty more.

The week after finding the White House saw me in New York and Los Angeles. I then went on trips to Berlin, Toronto and back to New York. I had several important commissions and I was completely absorbed in my undertakings. Yet always, even in the midst of a crowded auction room, or when with a client, on a plane or in a foreign hotel, always and however full my mind was of the job I was engaged upon, I seemed to have some small part of myself in which the memory of the small hand was fresh and immediate. It was almost like a room into which I could go for a moment or two during the day. I was not in the least alarmed or troubled by this. On the contrary, I found it oddly comforting.

I knew that when my present period of travel and activity was over I would return to it and try both to understand what had happened to me and if possible to return to that place to explore and to discover more about it – who had lived there, why it was empty. And whether, if I returned and stood there quietly, the small hand would seek mine again.

I had one disconcerting moment in an airport while buying a newspaper. It was extremely busy and as I queued, first of all someone pushed past me in a rush and almost sent me flying and then, as I was still recovering myself, I felt a child's hand take my own. But when I glanced down I saw that it was the real hand belonging to a real small boy who had clutched me in panic, having also been almost felled by the same precipitate traveller. Within a few seconds he had pulled away from me and was reunited with his mother. The feeling of his hand had been in a way just the same as that of the other child, but it had also been quite different – hot rather than cool, sticky rather than silky. I could not remember when a real child had last taken my hand but it must have been years before. Yet I could distinguish quite clearly between them.

It was mid-June before I had a break from travelling. I had had a profitable few weeks and among other things I had secured two rare Kelmscott Press books for my client in Sussex, together with immaculate signed first editions of all Virginia Woolf's novels, near-mint in their dust wrappers. I was excited to have them and anxious to get them out of my hands and into his. I am well insured, but no amount of money can compensate for the loss or damage of items like these.

So I arranged to drive down with them.

At the back of my mind was the idea that I would leave time to go in search of the White House again.

Three

Was there ever a June as glorious as that one? I had missed too much of the late spring but now we were in the heady days of balmy air and the first flush of roses. They were haymaking as I drove down and when I arrived at my client's house, the garden was lush and tumbling, the beds high and thick with flowers in full bloom, all was bees and honeysuckle and the smell of freshly mown grass.

I had been invited to stay the night and we dined on a terrace from which there was a distant view of the sea. Sir Edgar Merriman was elderly, modest of manner and incalculably rich. His tastes were for books and early scientific instruments and he also had a collection of rare musical boxes which, when wound and set going, charmed the evening air with their sound.

We lingered outside and Sir Edgar's blue-grey coils of cigar smoke wreathed upwards, keeping the insects at bay, the pungent smell mingling with that of the lilies and stocks in the nearby beds. His wife, Alice, sat with us, a small, grey-haired woman with a sweet voice and a shyness which I found most appealing.

At one point the servant came to call Sir Edgar to the telephone and as she and I sat companionably in the soft darkness, the moths pattering around the lamp, I thought to ask her about the White House. Did she know of it? Could she direct me to it again?

She shook her head. 'I haven't heard of such a place. How far were you from here?'

'It's hard to tell ... I was hopelessly lost. I suppose I'd driven for forty-five minutes or so? Perhaps a bit longer. I took a byroad which I thought I knew but did not.'

'There are so many unsigned roads in the country. We all know our way about so well, but they are a pitfall for the unwary. I don't think I can help you. Why do you want to go back there, Mr Snow?'

I had known them both for some four or five years

and stayed here overnight once or twice before, but to me they were always Sir Edgar and Lady Merriman and I was always Mr Snow, never Adam. I rather liked that.

I hesitated. What could I have said? That a deserted and half-derelict house and overgrown garden had some attraction for me, had almost put me under a spell so that I wanted to explore them further? That I was drawn back because ... how could I have told her about the small hand?

'Oh – you know how some old places have a strange attractiveness. And I might want to retire to the country some day.'

She said nothing and, after a moment, her husband returned and the conversation turned back to books and to what he had a mind to buy next. He had wide-ranging tastes and came up with some unusual suggestions. I was always challenged by him, always kept on my toes. He was an exciting client because I could never second-guess him.

'Do you know,' he asked now, passing me the decanter, 'if another First Folio of Shakespeare is ever likely to come up for sale?'

I almost knocked over my glass.

IT WAS HALF an hour later but the air was still warm as we gathered ourselves to go inside. I was fired with enthusiasm at the same time as I was coolly certain that no First Folio was likely to come my way for Sir Edgar. But even the speculative talk about it had made me think of his wealth in quite new terms.

As I was bidding him goodnight, Lady Merriman said suddenly, 'I think I have it, Mr Snow. I think I have the answer. Do just give me a moment if you would.' She went out of the room and I heard her footsteps going up the stairs and away into the depths of the house.

I sat in a low chair beside the open French windows. The lamp was out and a faint whiff of oil came from it. The sky was thick with stars.

And I asked in a low voice, 'Who *are* you?' For I had a strange sense of someone being there with me. But of course there was no one. I was alone and it was peaceful and calm.

Eventually, she returned carrying something.

'I am so sorry, Mr Snow. What we are looking for has always just been moved somewhere else. But this may possibly help you. It came to me as we were sitting there after dinner – the house. The name you gave, the White House, did not register with me because it was always known as Denny's House, to everyone locally – it is about twenty miles from here, but in the country that is local, you know.'

She sat down.

'You really shouldn't have gone to any trouble. It was a passing whim. I don't quite know now why it affected me.'

'There is an article about it in this magazine. It's rather old. We do keep far too much and I have quite a run of these. The house became known as Denny's House because it belonged to Denny Parsons. Have you heard the name?'

I shook my head.

'How quickly things fall away,' she said. 'You'll find everything about Denny Parsons and the garden in here.' She handed me a *Country Life* of some forty years ago. 'Something happened there but it was all hushed up. I don't know any more, I'm afraid. Now, do stay down for as long as you like, Mr Snow, but if you will excuse me, I am away to my bed.'

I went out on to the terrace for a last few moments. Everything had settled for the night, the stars were brilliant, and I thought I could just hear the faint hush of the sea as it folded itself over on the shingle.

IN MY ROOM I sat beside my open window with the sweet smell of the garden drifting in and read what Lady Merriman had found for me.

The article was about a remarkable and 'important' garden created at the White House by Mrs Denisa – apparently always known as Denny – Parsons and contained photographs of its creator strolling across lawns and pointing out this or that shrub, looking up into trees. There was also one of those dewy black-and-white portrait photographs popular in such magazines then, of Mrs Parsons in twinset and pearls, and holding a few delphiniums, rather awkwardly, as if uncertain whether or not to put them down. The soft focus made her look powdery and slightly vacant, but I could see through it to a handsome woman with strong features.

The story seemed straightforward. She had been widowed suddenly when her two children were nine and eleven years old and had decided to move from the Surrey suburbs into the country. When she had found the White House it had been empty and with an overgrown wilderness round it, out of which she had gradually made what was said in the reverential article to be 'one of the great gardens of our time'.

Then came extensive descriptions of borders

and walks and avenues, theatre gardens and knot gardens, of fountains and waterfalls and woodland gardens set beside cascading streams, with lists of flowers and shrubs, planting plans and diagrams and three pages of photographs. It certainly looked very splendid, but I am no gardener and was no judge of the relative 'importance' of Mrs Parsons's garden.

The place had become well known. People visited not only from miles away but from other countries. At the time the article was written it was 'open daily from Wednesday to Sunday for an entrance fee of one shilling and sixpence'.

The prose gushed on and I skimmed some of the more horticultural paragraphs. But I wanted to know more. I wanted to know what had happened next. Mrs Parsons had found a semi-derelict house in the middle of a jungle. The house in the photographs was handsome and in good order, with well-raked gravel and mown grass, fresh paint, open windows, at one of which a pale upstairs curtain blew out prettily on the breeze.

But the wheel had come full circle. When I had found the house and garden they were once again abandoned and decaying. That had happened to many a country house in the years immediately after the war but it was uncommon now.

I was not interested in the delights of herbaceous border and pleached lime. The house was handsome in the photographs, but I had seen it empty and half given over to wind and rain and the birds and was drawn by it as I would never have been by somewhere sunny and well presented.

I set the magazine down on the table. Things change after all, I thought, time does its work, houses are abandoned and sometimes nature reclaims what we have tried to make our own. The White House and garden had had their resurrection and a brief hour in the sun but their bright day was done now.

Yet as I switched out the lamp and lay listening to the soft soughing of the sea, I knew that I would have to go back. I had to find out more. I was not much interested in the garden and house. I wanted to know about the woman who had found it and rescued it yet apparently let it all slip through her fingers again. But most of all, of course, I wanted to go back because of the small hand.

Had Denny Parsons stood there in the gathering dusk, looking at the empty house, surrounded by that green wilderness, and as she made her plans for it felt the invisible small hand creep into her own?

Four

Nothing happened with any connection to the Merrimans or the part of the world in which they lived, and where I had come upon the White House, for several weeks. My trade was going through a dull patch. It happens every so often and ought not to trouble me, but after a short time without any requests from clients or phone calls about possible treasures I become nervous and irritable. If the dead patch continues for longer, I start wondering if I will have to sell some of my own few treasures, convinced that the bottom has dropped out of the business and I will never be active again. Every time it happens I remind myself that things have never failed to turn round, yet I never seem able to learn from experience.

I was not entirely idle of course. I bought and sold one or two complete library sets, including a first edition of Thomas Hardy, and even wondered whether to take up the request from an American collector to find him a full set of the James Bond first editions, mint and in dust wrappers, price immaterial. This is not my field, but I started to ask about in a desultory way, knowing I was probably the hundredth dealer the man had employed to find the Bonds and the one least likely to unearth them.

The summer began to stale. London emptied. I thought half-heartedly of visiting friends in Seattle.

And then two things happened on the same day.

In the post I received an envelope containing a card and a cutting from an old newspaper.

Mr Snow, I unearthed this clipping about the house, Denny's House, which you came upon by chance when getting lost on your way to us in June. I thought perhaps you might still be interested as it tells a little story. I am sure there is more and if I either remember or read about it again I will let you know. But please throw this away if it is no longer of interest. Just a thought.

Sincerely, Alice Merriman.

I poured a second cup of coffee and picked up the yellowed piece of newspaper.

There was a photograph of a woman whom I recognised as Denisa Parsons, standing beside a large ornamental pool with a youngish man. In the centre of the pool was a bronze statue at which they were looking in the slightly artificial manner of all posed photographs. The statue was of a young boy playing with a dolphin and a golden ball and rose quite beautifully out of the still surface of the water, on which there were one or two water lilies. There might have been fish but none was visible.

The news item was brief. The statue had been commissioned by Denisa Parsons in memory of her grandson, James Harrow, who had been drowned in what was simply described as 'a tragic accident'. The man with her was the sculptor, whose name was not familiar to me, and the statue was now in place at 'Mrs Parsons's internationally famous White House garden'. That was all, apart from a couple of lines about the sculptor's other work.

I looked at the photograph for some time but I could read nothing into the faces, with their rather public smiles, and although the sculpture looked charming to me, I am no art critic.

I put the cutting in a drawer of my desk, sent Lady

Merriman a postcard of thanks and then forgot about the whole thing, because by the same post had come a letter from an old friend at the Bodleian Library telling me that he thought he might have news of a Shakespeare First Folio which could conceivably be for sale. If I would like to get in touch …

Fifteen minutes later I was in a taxi on my way to Paddington station to catch the next train to Oxford.

Five

haven't had an extended lunch break for, what, five years? So I'm taking one today.'

It did not surprise me. I have known quite a few librarians across the world, in major libraries and senior posts, and none has ever struck me as likely to take a long lunch, or even in some cases a lunch at all. It is not their way. So I was delighted when Fergus McCreedy, a very senior man at the Bodleian, suggested we walk from there up to lunch at the Old Parsonage. It was a warm, bright summer's day and Oxford was, as ever, crowded. But in August its crowds are different. Parties of tourists trail behind their guide, who holds up a red umbrella or a pom-pom on a stick so as not to lose any of his charges and language-school students on bicycles replace undergraduates on the same. Otherwise, Oxford is Oxford. I always enjoy returning to my old city, so long as I stay no more than a couple of days. Oxford has a way of making one feel old.

Fergus never looks old. Fergus is ageless. He will look the same when he is ninety as he did the day I met him, when we were both eighteen and in our first week at Balliol. He has never left Oxford and he never will. He married a don, Helena, a world expert on some aspect of early Islamic art, they live in a tiny, immaculate house in a lane off the lower Woodstock Road, they take their holidays in countries like Jordan and Turkistan. They have no children, but if they ever did, those children would be, as so many children of Oxford academics have always been, born old.

I had not seen Fergus for a couple of years. We had plenty to catch on up during our walk to lunch and later while we enjoyed a first glass of wine at our quiet table in the Old Parsonage's comfortable dining room. But when our plates of potted crab arrived, I asked Fergus about his letter.

'As you know, I have a very good client who has set me some difficult challenges in the past few years. I have usually found what he wanted – he's a very knowledgeable book collector. It's a pleasure to work with him.'

'Not one of the get-me-anything-so-long-as-it-costs-a-lot brigade, then.'

'Absolutely not. I have no idea how much he's worth or how he made his money, but it doesn't signify, Fergus, because he loves his books. He's a reader as well as a collector. He appreciates what I find for him. I know I have a living to earn and money is money, but there are some I could barely bring myself to work for.'

I meant it. I had had an appalling couple of years being retained by a Russian oil billionaire who only wanted a book if it was publicised as being both extremely rare and extremely expensive and who did not even want to take delivery of what I bought for him. Everything went straight into a bank vault.

'So your man wants a First Folio.'

Our rare fillet of beef, served cold with a new potato and asparagus salad, was set down and we ordered a second glass of Fleurie.

'I told him it was more or less impossible. They're all in libraries.'

'We have three,' Felix said. 'The Folger has around eighty. Getty bought one a few years ago of course – that was sold by one of our own colleges.'

'Oriel. Yes. Great shame.'

Felix shrugged. 'They needed the money more than the book. I can understand that. A small private library in London with a mainly theological collection, Dr Williams's Library, sold its copy a year or so back for two and a half million. But that endows the rest of their collection and saves it for the foreseeable future. It's a question of balancing one thing against another.'

'If you had a First Folio would you sell it?'

Felix smiled. 'The one I have in mind as being just possibly for sale does not belong to me. Nor to the Bodleian.'

'I thought every one of the 230 or so copies was accounted for?'

'Almost every one. It was thought for some years that apart from all those on record in libraries and colleges and a few in private hands, there was one other First Folio, somewhere in India. But almost by chance, and by following up a few leads, I think I have discovered that that is not the case.'

He helped himself to more salad. The room had filled. I looked at the walls, which were lined with an extraordinary assortment of pictures, oils and watercolours, five deep in places – none of them was of major importance but every single one had merit and charm. The collection enhanced the pleasant room considerably.

'The Folio was mentioned to me in passing,' Fergus said, 'because my German colleague was emailing me about something entirely different, which we have been trying to track down for a long time – a medieval manuscript in fact. In the course of a conversation I had with Dieter, he said almost in passing something like, "They don't know half of what they do possess, including a Shakespeare First Folio."'

'They?' I said.

Fergus got up. 'Shall we have our coffee on the terrace? I see the sun has come out again.'

꜀

SITTING AT A TABLE under a large awning, we were somewhat protected from the noise of the passing traffic on the Banbury Road and the coffee was first-rate.

Fergus took three gulps of his double espresso. 'Have you ever heard of the monastery of Saint Mathieu des Etoiles?'

'I didn't so much as know there was such a saint.'

'Not many do. He's pretty obscure, though there are a couple of churches in France dedicated to him, but so far as I know only one monastery bears his name. It's Cistercian, an enclosed and silent order, and very remote indeed, a bit like La Grande Trappe – high up among mountains and forests, in its own small pocket of time. In winter it can be completely cut off. There is a village some six miles away, but otherwise it's as remote from civilisation as you can probably get anywhere in Western Europe. Oh and it also maintains the tradition of wonderful sacred music. A few people do visit – for the music, for a retreat – and the monastery is surprisingly in touch with what you might call our world.'

'Most of them are,' I said. 'I know one in the Appalachian Mountains – remote as they come, but they are on email.'

'When you think about it, the silent email suits the rule far better than the telephone. Now, a couple of years ago I had the good fortune to visit Saint Mathieu. They have one of the finest and oldest and best-preserved monastic libraries in the world. One of the ways they earn their living is in book restoration and rebinding for other libraries. We've used their skills occasionally. You're wondering what all this has to do with you? More coffee?'

We ordered. The terrace was emptying out now, as lunchtime drew to a close.

'The monastery, like so many, is in need of money for repairs. When your building dates from the twelfth century things start to wear out. They are not a rich order and the work they do keeps them going, but without anything over and to spare. They urgently need repairs to the chapel frescoes and the roof of the great chapter house, and even though they will provide some of the labour themselves, the monks can't do it all – they don't have the skills and, besides, many of them are in their seventies and older. So, after a great deal of difficulty, they have obtained permission to sell one or two treasures – mainly items which don't have much reason to be there, and which sit rather oddly in a Cistercian monastery. For instance, for some strange reason they have one or two early Islamic items.'

'Ah – so Helena comes into the picture.'

'She does. So do we. They have a couple of medieval manuscripts, for instance – an Aelfric, a Gilbert of Hoyland. In each case it was thought only one or possibly two copies existed in the world, but Saint Mathieu turns out to have wonderful examples. They only need to sell a few things to pay for all of their repairs and rebuilding and to provide an endowment against future depredations. They're pretty prone to weather damage up there, apart from anything else. They need to protect themselves against future extreme winters.'

'It's pretty unusual for items like this to come on the market, Fergus. What else have they got? You make me want to get on the next plane.'

He held up his hand. 'No. "The market" is exactly what they do not want to know about any of this. They made contact with us under a seal of total confidentiality. I'm not supposed to be talking to you, so I'd be obliged if you said nothing either.'

I was put out. Why tell me at all if my hands were going to be tied as well as my lips sealed?

'Don't sulk.' Fergus looked at me shrewdly. 'I haven't mentioned this to anyone and I don't intend to – apart from anything else, there would be no point. But the thing is, they have a Shakespeare First Folio – one that was supposed to be somewhere in India. It has never been properly accounted for and my view is that it isn't in India at all but in the Monastery of Saint Mathieu des Etoiles.'

'How on earth did they acquire it?'

He shrugged. 'Who knows? But in the past when rich young men entered the monastery as postulants their families gave a sort of dowry and it sometimes took the form of art treasures, rare books and so on, as well as of money. That's probably what happened in this case.'

'Do they know what they've got?'

'Pretty much. They're neither fools nor inno-cents. And they are certainly not to be cheated. No, I know you would not, Adam, but your trade is as open to charlatans as any other.'

'I like the way you call it "my" trade.'

'Oh, don't look at me,' Fergus said, smiling slightly. 'I'm just a simple librarian.' He stood up. 'I've extended my lunch hour far enough. Are you walking back into town?'

He paid the bill and we turned out of the gate and began to walk towards St Giles.

'The thing is,' Fergus said, 'some of the items they might conceivably sell will go to America – we simply don't have the money in this country. I am talking to a couple of potential private benefactors but I don't hold out much hope – they get talked to by the world and his wife. Why should they want to give us a single priceless medieval manuscript when they could build the wing of a hospital or endow a chair in medical research? I can't blame them. We've already got First Folios. So have the other libraries. We none of us need another. But you have a client who could presumably afford three or four million to get what he wants?'

'He would never have mentioned it to me if he

didn't know how unlikely I was to get one for him, how much it might cost if I ever did and that he could well afford that. He's a gentleman.'

'Ah, one of those. Would you like me to get in touch with the monastery and ask one or two discreet questions? I won't mention your name or anything of that kind – and I'll have to work up to it. I think I have the way of them now, but I don't want to pounce or the portcullis will come down.'

'And they'll be off to the Huntington Library in a trice.'

Fergus's mouth firmed slightly. I laughed.

'You'd all stab one another in the back just as surely as we dealers would,' I said. 'But thank you, Fergus. And of course, please put in a word. Whatever it takes.'

'Yes,' he said. 'Don't call us and all that.'

We parted outside Bodley, Fergus to go in to his eyrie beyond the Duke Humfrey Library, while I went on towards the High. It was a beautiful day now, the air clear and warm, a few clouds like smoke rings high in the sky. There were plenty of trains back to London but I was in no hurry. I thought I would walk down to one of my old favourite haunts, the Botanic Garden, which is surely Oxford's best-kept secret.

Six

I went in through the great gate and began to walk slowly down the wide avenue, looking about me with pleasure, remembering many a happy hour spent here. But it was the Cistercian monastery of Saint Mathieu des Etoiles and its library, as well as the possibility of acquiring a very rare book indeed, which were at the front of my mind. I knew that I could not speak a word of what Fergus had told me, not to Sir Edgar Merriman, nor to a single other soul. I was not such a fool and, besides, I rather wanted to prove to Fergus that antiquarian book dealers are not all charlatans. But I was sure that he had been half-teasing. He knew me well enough.

I wondered how long it would take him to oil his

way round to mention of the First Folio in his correspondence with the monastery – presumably by email,
as he had hinted. Perhaps not long at all. Perhaps in
a day or so I might know whether the business was
going to move a step further forward or whether the
subject of the Folio would be scotched immediately.
There was absolutely nothing I could do but wait.

I had come to the great round lily pond which
attends at the junction of several paths. Three or
four people were sitting on the benches in the semi-
circle beside it, enjoying the sunshine. One woman
was reading a book, another was knitting. A younger
one had a pram in which a baby was sound asleep.

I sat at the end of a bench, still thinking about the
Folio, but as I sat, something happened. It is very
hard to describe, though it is easy enough to remember. But I had never known any sensation like it and
I can feel it still.

I should stress again how at ease I was. I had had
a good lunch with an old friend, who had given me
a piece of potentially very exciting information. I
was in one of my favourite cities, which holds only
happy memories for me. The sun was shining. All
was right with the world, in fact.

The young woman with the pram had just got up,
checked on her baby and strolled off back towards

the main gate, leaving the reader, the knitter and me in front of the raised stone pool in which the water lay dark and shining and utterly still.

And at that moment I felt the most dreadful fear. It was not fear of anything, it was simply fear, fear and dread, like a coldness rising up through my body, gripping my chest so that I felt I might not be able to breathe, and stiffening the muscles of my face as if they were frozen. I could feel my heart pounding inside my ribcage, and the waves of its beat roaring through my ears. My mouth was dry and it seemed that my tongue was cleaving to the roof of my mouth. My upper lip and jaw, my neck and shoulder and the whole of my left side felt as if they were being squeezed in a vice and for a split second I believed that I was having a heart attack, except that I felt no pain, and after a second or two the grip eased a little, though it was still hard to breathe. I stood up and began to gasp for air, and I felt my body, which had been as if frozen cold, begin to flush and then to sweat. I was terrified. But of what, of what? Nothing had happened. I had seen nothing, heard nothing. The day was as sunlit as before, the little white clouds sailed carelessly in the sky and one or two of them were reflected in the surface of the still pool.

And then I felt something else. I had an

overwhelming urge to go close to the pool, to stand beside the stone rim and peer into the water. I realised what was happening to me. Some years ago, Hugo, my brother and older than me by six years, went through a mental breakdown from which it took him a couple of years to recover. He had told me that in the weeks before he was forced to seek medical help and, indeed, to be admitted to hospital, almost the worst among many dreadful experiences was of feeling an overwhelming urge to throw himself off the edge of the underground station platform into the path of a train. When he was so afraid of succumbing to its insistence he walked everywhere, he felt he must step off the pavement into the path of the traffic. He stayed at home, only to be overwhelmed again, this time by the urge to throw himself out of the window onto the pavement below.

And now it was happening to me. I felt as if I was being forced forward by a power outside myself. And what this power wanted me to do was throw myself face down into the great deep pool. As I felt the push from behind so I felt a powerful magnetic force pulling me forward. The draw seemed to be coming from the pool itself and between the two forces I was totally powerless. I think that I was split seconds from flinging myself forward into and under the dark water when the woman who had been knitting suddenly started up, flapping at a wasp. Her movement broke the spell and I felt everything relax, the power shrink and shrivel back, leaving me standing in the middle of the path, a yard or so from the pool. A couple were walking towards me, hand in hand. A light aircraft puttered slowly overhead. A breeze blew.

Slowly, slowly, the fear drained out of me, though I felt shaken and light-headed, so that I backed away and sat down again on the bench to recover myself.

I stayed for perhaps twenty minutes. It took as long as this for me to feel calm again. As I sat there in the sunshine, I thought of Hugo. I had never fully understood until now how terrifying his ordeal had been, and how the terrors must have taken him over, mentally and physically. No wonder he had said to me when I first visited him in the hospital that he felt safe for the first time in several years.

Was it hereditary, then? Was I about to experience these terrifying urges to throw myself out of windows or into the path of oncoming trains? I knew that Hugo had gone through a very turbulent time in his youth and I had put his condition down to a deep-seated reaction to that. So far as I knew, neither of our parents had ever suffered in the same way.

At last, I managed to get up and walk towards the gates. I felt better with every step. The fear was receding rapidly. I only shivered slightly as I looked back at the pool. Nothing more.

I was glad to be in the bustle of the High and I had no urge whatsoever to throw myself under a bus. I walked briskly to the railway station and caught the next train back to London.

THAT NIGHT I DREAMED that I was swimming underwater, among shimmering fish with gold and silver iridescent bodies which glided past me and around me in the cool, dark water. For a while, it was beautiful. I felt soothed and lulled. I thought I heard faint music. But then I was no longer swimming, I was drowning. I had seemed to be like a fish myself, able to breathe beneath the surface, but suddenly the air was being pressed out of my lungs by a fast inflow of water and I was gasping, with a painful sensation in my chest and a dreadful pulsing behind my eyes.

I came to in the darkness of my bedroom, reached out to switch on the lamp and then sat, taking in great draughts of air. I got up and went to the window, opened it and breathed in the cool London night, and the smell of the trees and grass in the communal gardens of the square. I supposed the panic which had overcome me beside the pool in the Botanic Garden had inevitably left its traces in my subconscious, so that it was not surprising these had metamorphosed into night horrors.

But it faded quickly, just as the terror of the afternoon had faded. I am generally of an equable temperament and I was restored to my normal spirits quite easily. I was only puzzled that I should have had such an attack of panic out of the blue, followed by a nightmare from which I had surfaced thrashing in fear. I had had a pleasant day and I was excited about Fergus's possible coup. The tenor of my life was as even and pleasant as always.

The only untoward thing that had happened to me recently was the incident in the garden of the White House. Unlike the terror and the nightmare, the memory of that had not faded – indeed, if anything it was clearer. I closed my eyes and felt again the small hand in mine. I could almost fold my fingers over it, so real, so vivid was the sensation.

Without quite knowing that I was going to do so then, I did fold my fingers over as if to enclose it. But there was nothing.

Not this time. Not tonight.

Seven

My business was going through the usual summer lull and I did not have enough to occupy me. The nightmare did not return, but although I had no more attacks of fear, I could not get that experience out of my mind and, in the end, I decided that I would talk to my brother. I rang to ask if I could go to see them for a night and got his Danish wife, Benedicte, who was always welcoming. I think that so far as she was concerned I could have turned up on their doorstep at any time of the day or night and I would have been welcome. With Hugo, though, it was different.

He was now a teacher in a boys' public school situated in a pleasant market town in Suffolk. They had a Georgian house with a garden running down to the river and the slight air of being out of time that always seems to be part of such places.

They had one daughter, Katerina, who had just left to stay with her cousins in Denmark for the holiday. Hugo and Benedicte were going to the States, where he was to teach a summer school.

I have always felt a great calm and contentment as I step through their front door. The house is light and elegant and always immaculate. But if it belongs to the eighteenth century from the outside, within it is modern Scandinavian, with a lot of pale wood flooring, cream rugs, cream leather chairs, steel and chrome. It would be soulless were it not for two things. The warmth that emanates from Benedicte herself, and the richly coloured wall hangings which she weaves and sells. They make the house sing with scarlet and regal purple, deep blue and emerald.

It is a strange environment for my brother. Hugo has perhaps never quite picked up the last threads of equilibrium, which is why the house and his wife are so good for him. He has an edginess, a tendency to disappear inside himself and look into some painful distance, detached from what is going on around him. But he loves his job and his family and I do not think he is greatly troubled – for all that he has re-minders of his sufferings from time to time.

I ARRIVED IN the late afternoon and caught up on news. Benedicte was going out to her orchestra practice – she plays the oboe – but left us with a delicious dinner which needed only a few final touches put to it. The kitchen opened on to the garden, with a distant glimpse of the river, and it was warm enough for us to have the doors open on to a still evening. The flames of the candles in their slender silver holders scarcely flickered.

'I need your advice,' I said to Hugo, as we began to eat our smoked fish. 'Advice, help – I'm really not sure which.'

He looked across at me. We are not alike. Hugo takes after our mother, in being tall and dark with a long oval face. I am stockier and fairer, though we are of a height. But our eyes are the same, a deep smoky blue. Looking into Hugo's eyes was oddly like looking into my own in a mirror. How much else of his depths might I see in myself, I wondered.

'Do you ever …' I looked at the fish on my fork. I did not know how to ask, what words to use that would not upset him. 'I wonder if you sometimes …'

He was looking straight at me, the blue eyes direct

and as unwavering as the candle flames. But he was silent. He gave me no help.

'The thing is … something quite nasty happened to me. Nothing like it has ever happened before. Not to me. Nothing …' I heard my voice trailing off into silence.

After a moment Hugo said, 'Go on.'

As if a torrent had been unleashed, I began to tell him about the afternoon in the Botanic Garden and my terrible fear and then the overwhelming urge to fall face down into the water. I told him everything about the day, I elaborated on my feelings leading up to the fear, I went into some detail about how things were in my present life. The only thing I did not mention, because there were somehow not the words to describe it, was the small hand.

Hugo listened without interrupting. We helped ourselves to chicken pie. A salad.

I fell silent. Hugo took a piece of bread. Outside it had grown quite dark. It was warm. It was very still. I remembered the night I had sat out on the terrace at the Merrimans' house in the gathering dusk, so soon after these strange events had begun.

'And you think you are going mad,' Hugo said evenly. 'Like me.'

'No. Of course I don't.'

'Oh, come on, Adam … If you're here to get my advice or whatever it is you want, tell me the truth.'

'I'm sorry. But the truth is – well, I don't know what it is, but you didn't go mad.'

'Yes, I did. Whatever "mad" is, I went it to some degree. I was in a madhouse, for God's sake.'

I had never heard him speak so harshly.

'Sorry,' I said.

'It's fine. I hardly think about it now. It's long gone. Yet there is sometimes the shadow of a shadow, and when that happens I wonder if it could come back. And I don't know, because I don't know what caused it in the first place. My psyche was turned inside out and shaken, but they never got to the bottom of why.'

He looked at me speculatively. 'So now you.' Then, seeing my expression, he added quickly, 'Sorry, Adam. Of course not you. What you had was just a panic attack.'

'But I've never had such a thing in my life.'

He shrugged. A great, soft, pale moth had come in through the open window and was pattering round the lamp. I have never cared for moths.

'Let's go out for some air,' I said.

It was easier, strolling beside my brother down the garden. I could talk without having to see his face.

'Why would I have what you call a panic attack, out of the blue? What would cause it?'

'I've no idea. Perhaps you're not well?'

'I'm perfectly well.'

'Shouldn't you see your GP all the same, get a check?'

'I suppose I could. When you …'

'No,' he said, 'I wasn't ill either.'

We stood at the bottom of the path. A few paces away was the dark river.

'I was within a hair's breadth of throwing myself into that pool. It was terrifying. It was as if I had to do it, something was making me.'

'Yes.'

'I'm afraid it will happen again.'

He put a hand briefly on my shoulder. 'Go and see someone. But it probably won't, you know.'

'Did you ever ask if anyone else in the family had had these – attacks, these fears?'

'Yes. So far as anyone knew, they didn't.'

'Oh.'

'I think that part really is coincidence.'

'I might not be able to resist another time.'

'I'm pretty sure you will.'

'Might you have jumped in front of one of those trains?'

'I think ...' he said carefully, 'that there was usually something inside me that held me back – something stronger than it, whatever "it" was. But once ... once perhaps.' He shook himself. 'I'd rather not.'

'The shadow of a shadow.'

'Yes.'

We heard the sound of Benedicte's car pulling up and then the bang of the front door. Hugo turned to go back inside. I did not. I walked on, beyond the end of the garden and across the narrow path until I was standing on the riverbank. I could smell the water, and although there was only a half-moon, the surface of it shone faintly. I felt calm now, calm and relieved. Hugo seemed to have come through his own ordeal unscathed. He did not want to dwell on it and I couldn't blame him. I think I knew that whatever had happened to me was of a different order and with a quite different origin. I also knew that if ever it happened to me again, my brother would not want to help me. Nothing had been said and in all other respects I knew I would always be able to rely on him, as I hoped he would upon me. But in this, I was alone.

Or perhaps not alone.

I heard the water lap the side of the bank softly. I felt no fear of it. Why should I?

I waited for some time there in the darkness. I heard their voices from the house. A door closed. A light went on upstairs.

I waited until I felt the night chill off the water and then I turned away with what I realised was a sort of sadness, a disappointment that the small hand had not crept into mine. I was coming to expect it.

I still had the sense then that the hand belonged to someone whose intentions were wholly benign and who was well disposed towards me, who was trusting.

I WAS TO look back on that night with longing – longing for the sense of peace I knew then, even if I also felt an odd sudden loneliness; even if I had, God help me, for some strange reason actually hoped for the presence of the small hand holding mine.

Eight

The following night I had another vivid dream. I was standing as I had stood that evening beside the broken-down gate that led into the garden of the White House, only this time it was not evening but night, a cold, clear night with a sky sown with glittering stars. I was alone and I was waiting. I knew that I was waiting but for whom I waited the dream did not tell me. I felt excited, keyed up, as if some longed-for excitement was about to happen or I was to see something very beautiful, experience some great pleasure.

After a time, I knew that someone was coming towards me from the depths of the garden beyond the gate, though I neither heard nor saw anything.

But there was a small light bobbing in the darkness among the trees and bushes some way ahead and I knew that it was getting nearer. Perhaps someone was carrying a lantern.

I waited. In a moment, whoever it was would appear or call out to me. I was eager to see them. They were bringing me something – not an object but some news or information. They were going to tell me something and when they had told me, everything would fall into place. I would know a great secret.

The light disappeared now and then, as the undergrowth obscured it, but then I saw it again a little nearer to me. I moved a step or two forward, my hand on the broken gate. I can feel it now, the cool roughened wood under my palm. I can see the lamp growing a little brighter.

I felt a great wave of happiness and, at the same time, a desire to run towards the light, to push my way roughly through the branches that hung low over the path. I had to do so. I was needed. It was urgent that I should go into the garden, that I should meet the lantern-bearer, that I should not waste another moment, as I somehow felt that I had wasted so many – not moments, but months and years.

I pushed on the gate to try and free it from where

it was embedded in the earth and grass, which had grown up in great coarse clumps around it.

I was not pushing hard enough. The gate did not budge. I put my shoulder to it. I had to open it and go into the garden, go quickly, because now the light was very near but going crazily from side to side, as if someone was swinging it hard.

I put my whole strength to the gate and pushed. It gave suddenly so that I was pitched forward and felt myself falling.

And as I fell, I woke.

❧

I THOUGHT A GREAT deal about the dream in the course of the next couple of days and instead of fading from my mind the memory of it became stronger. Perhaps if I could find out more about the White House and its garden, and if I went there again, I would be able to loosen the strange hold it seemed to have on me.

I would pay a visit to the London Library, and if that yielded nothing the library of the RHS, and try to find anything that had been written about it. I had no interest in gardens but something had led me to the ruins of that one and something had happened to

51

me during those few minutes I had spent there which was haunting me now.

Before I had a chance to get to any library, however, a phone call from Fergus McCreedy put the whole matter from my mind.

'I have news for you,' he said.

༄

THE MONASTERY OF Saint Mathieu des Etoiles clearly trusted Fergus. The Librarian had sent him a confidential list of the treasures they felt able to sell to raise the money they needed. They included, he said, two icons, the Islamic objects in which Helena was so interested, and three medieval manuscripts. And a Shakespeare First Folio. The Librarian had asked Fergus if he would act as go-between in the disposal of the items – they wanted someone who had an entrée to libraries, museums and collectors round the world, who could be trusted not to send out a press release, and above all a man they regarded as fair and honourable. Fergus was to visit the monastery later in the summer, to look at everything, but he had proposed that I be allowed to go there at once, specifically to look at the First Folio. He had told the Librarian about me. My credentials seemed to satisfy and Fergus suggested I make arrangements with the monastery to visit as soon as I could. If I agreed, he proposed to forward all the contact details.

'It is a silent order,' he said, 'but the Librarian and the Guest Master are allowed to talk in the course of their duties, and both speak English. I suggest you get on with it.'

I asked if that meant he thought they might change their minds.

'Not at all. It has been deliberated over for a long time. They are quite sure and the Head of the Order has approved it all. But you don't want anyone else to get wind of this and neither do I. In my experience things have a way of getting out, even from enclosed orders of silent monks.'

Nine

I started on my journey in a mood of cheerfulness and optimism. The shadows had blown away. The sun had come out. I needed a break, which was why I flew to Lyons and then hired a car, for I planned to take my time, meandering on country roads, staying for two or three nights in different small towns and villages, enjoying France. I knew parts of the country well but not the region in which the monastery of Saint Mathieu des Etoiles was situated, high up in the mountains of the Vercors. I was ready to explore, pleased to be going on what I thought of as a pleasant jaunt and with the prospect of discovering a rare and wonderful book to delight a client at the end of it.

I hardly recognise the person I was at the beginning of that journey. It is true I had had a strange encounter and been touched by some shadow, but I had pushed them to the back of my mind; they had not changed me as I was later to be changed. I was able to forget. Now, I cannot.

I see those few days in a sunlit France as being days of light before the darkness, days of tranquillity and calm before the gathering storm. Days of innocence, perhaps.

It was high summer and hot, but the air was clear and, as always in such weather, the countryside looked its best, welcoming and uplifting to the spirits. There were pastures and gentle hills, charming villages. One night I had a room above an old stable in which chickens scratched contentedly and swallows were nesting. In the morning, I woke to lie looking across a distant line of violet-coloured hills. I was heading towards them that day. They seemed like pictures in a child's book.

I ate modestly at breakfast and lunch, but always stopped in time to dine well, so that I slept seven or eight hours, deep draughts of dreamless sleep.

By the time I was on the road for the third morning, the weather had begun to change. The sun shone for the first half-hour or so, but as I climbed higher I drove into patches of thin, swirling mist. It was very humid and I could see dark and heavy clouds gathering around the mountains ahead. Earlier, I had driven through many a small and pleasant village and seen people about, in the streets, working in the fields, cycling, walking, but now I was leaving human habitations behind. Several times I passed small roadside shrines, commemorating the wartime dead of the Resistance, which had been so strong in these parts. Once, an old woman was putting fresh flowers into the metal vase clipped to one of them. I waved to her. She stared but did not respond.

The roads became steeper and the bends sharper. The clouds were darkening. I passed through several short tunnels cut from the rock. On either side of me, the cliffs began to tower up, granite grey with only the odd fern or tree root clinging to its foothold. The car stuttered once or twice and I needed all my concentration to steer round some of the bends that coiled like snakes, up and up.

But then I came out on to a narrow plateau. The sky was darkening but to my right a thin blade of sunlight shot for a second down through the valley below. Somewhere, it caught water and the water gleamed. But then great drops of rain began to fall and a zigzag of blue-white lightning ran down the side of the rock. I was unsure whether to wait or to press on, but the road was narrow and I could not safely pull in to the side. I had not seen another vehicle for several miles but if one came up behind me, especially in the darkness and now blinding rain of the storm, it would certainly crash into me. I drove on extremely slowly. The rain was slanting sideways so that my windscreen was strangely clear. More lightning and still more streaking down the sulphurous-looking sky and arcing onto the road. I could not tell whether what was roaring on the car roof was rain or thunder.

The road was still narrow but now, instead of climbing I began to descend, skirting the highest part of the mountain and heading towards several lower slopes, their sides thickly overgrown with pine trees.

The rain was at my back and seemed to be coming out of a whirlwind which drove the car forward.

I am a perfectly calm driver and I had driven in atrocious conditions before then, but now I was afraid. The narrowness of the road, the way the storm and the high rocks seemed to be pressing down upon me at once, together with the tremendous noise, combined to unnerve me almost completely. I was conscious that I was alone, perhaps for many miles, and that although I had a map I had been warned that the monastery was difficult to find. I thought I had perhaps another twenty miles to go before I turned off on the track that led to Saint Mathieu, but I might well miss it in such weather.

Two things happened then.

Once again, in the midst of that black, swirling storm, a blade of sunlight somehow pierced its way through the dense cloud. This time I almost mistook it for another flash of lightning as it slanted down the rock face to my left and across the road ahead, which had the astonishing effect of turning the teeming rain into a thousand fragments of rainbow colours. It lasted for only a second or two before the clouds overwhelmed it again, but it was during those seconds that I saw the child. I was driving slowly. The road was awash and I could not see far ahead. But the child was there. I had no doubt of that then. I have no doubt of it now.

One moment there was only rain, bouncing up off the road surface, pouring down the steep sides of the cliff beside the car. Then, in the sudden shaft of sunlight, there was the child. He seemed to run down a narrow track at the side of the road between some overhanging trees and dash across in front of me. I braked, swerved, shouted, all at the same moment. The car slid sideways and came to a halt at the roadside, nose towards the rocks. I leaped out, disregarding the rain and the storm still raging overhead. I did not see how I could have avoided hitting the child, it had been so near to me, though I had felt no impact. I had not seen him – I was sure that it was a boy – fall but surely he must have done so. Perhaps he was beneath the car, lying injured.

Such violent storms blow themselves out very quickly in the mountains and I could see the veils of rain sweeping away from the valley ahead and it grew lighter as the clouds lifted. The thunder cracked above me but the lightning was less vivid now.

One glance under the car told me that the body of the child was not lying in the road beneath it. There was no mark on the front.

I looked round. I saw the track between the pine trees down which he must have come running. So he had raced in front of the car, missing it by inches, and presumably down some path on the opposite side.

I crossed the road. The thunder grumbled away to my right. Steam began to rise from the surface of the road and wisps of cloud drifted across in front of me like ectoplasm.

'Where are you?' I shouted. 'Are you all right?

Call to me.' I shouted again, this time in French.

I was standing on a patch of rough grass a few yards away from the car on the opposite side. Behind rose the jagged bare surface of rock. I turned and looked down. I was standing on the edge of a precipice. Below me was a sheer drop to a gorge below. I glimpsed dark water and the cliffs on the far side before I stepped back in terror. As I stepped, I missed my footing and almost fell but managed to right myself and leap across the road towards the safety of the car. As I did so, I felt quite unmistakably the small hand in mine. But this time it was not nestling gently within my own, it held me in a vicious grip and as it held so I felt myself pulled towards the edge of the precipice. It is difficult to describe how determined and relentless the urging of the hand was, how powerful the force of something I could not see. The strength was that of a grown man although the hand was still that of a child and at the same time as I was pulled I felt myself in some strange way being urged, coaxed, guided to the edge. If I could not be taken by force, then it was as though I were to be seduced to the precipice and into the gorge below.

The storm had rolled away now and the air was thick with moisture which hung heavily about me so that I could hardly breathe. I could hear the sound of rushing water and the rumble of stones down the hillside not far away. The torrent must have dislodged something higher up. I was desperate to get back into the safety of the car but I could not shake off the hand. What had happened to the child I could not imagine, but I had seen no pathway and if he had leaped, then he must have fallen. But where had a child come from in this desolate and empty landscape and in the middle of such a storm, and how had he managed to avoid being hit by my car and disappear over the edge of a precipice?

I wrenched my hand as hard as I could out of the grip of the invisible one. I felt as if I were resisting a great magnetic force, but somehow I stumbled backwards across the road and then managed to free my hand and get into the car. I slammed the door behind me in panic and, as I slammed it, I heard a howl. It was a howl of pain and rage and anguish combined, and without question the howl of a furious child.

Ten

My map was inadequate and there were no signs. I was shaking as I drove and had to keep telling myself that whatever might have happened, I had not killed or injured any child nor allowed myself to be lured over the precipice to my death. The storm was over but the day did not recover its spirits. The sky remained leaden, the air vaporous. From time to time, the curtain of cloud came down, making visibility difficult. Twice I took a wrong turning and was forced to find a way of re-tracing my route. I saw no one except a solitary man leading a herd of goats across a remote field.

After an hour and a half, I rounded a sharp bend, drove through one of the many tunnels cut into the rock and then saw a turning to the left, beside another of the little shrines. I stopped and consulted my map. If this was not the way to the monastery, I would press on another six miles to the next village and find someone to ask.

The narrow lane ran between high banks and through gloomy pine trees whose slender trunks rose up ahead and on either side of my car, one after another after another. After being level for some way, it began to twist and climb, and then to descend before climbing again. Then, quite suddenly, I came out into a broad clearing. Ahead of me was a small wooden sign surmounted by a cross: MONASTERE DE SAINT MATHIEU DES ETOILES. VOITURES.

I switched off the engine and got out of the car. The smell of moist earth and pine needles was intense. Now and again a few raindrops rolled down the tree trunks and pattered onto the ground. Thunder grumbled but it was some distance away. Otherwise, everything was silent. And I was transported back on the instant to the evening I had stood outside the gate of the White House and its secret, overgrown garden. I had the same sense of strangeness and isolation from the rest of the world.

I was expected at the monastery. I had had email correspondence with the Librarian and been assured that a guest room would be made available for me at any time. They had very few visitors and those mainly monks from other houses. The Librarian, Dom Martin, had attached a helpful set of notes about the monastery and its way of life. I would be able to speak only to him and (although it was possible I would also be received by the Abbot), to the Guest Master, might attend the services in the chapel and would be given access to the library. But this was an enclosed and silent order and, though I was welcome, I would be kept within bounds.

'C'est probable,' the Librarian had written, 'que vous serez ici tout seul.'

Now I took my bag from the car and set off down the narrow path through the dense and silent pines. I was still suffering from the effects of what had happened, but I was glad to have arrived at a place of safety where there would be other human beings, albeit silent and for the most part unapproachable. A monastery was holy ground. Surely nothing bad could happen to me here.

The track wound on for perhaps half a mile and for most of the way it was monotonous, rows of pines giving way to yet more. At first it was level, then I began to climb, and then to climb quite steeply. The only sound was the soft crunch of my own footsteps on the pine-needle floor. There were no birds, though in the distance I could hear falling water, as if a stream were tumbling down over rocks. The air was humid but as I climbed higher it cleared and even felt chill, which was a welcome relief. I imagined this place in deep winter, when the snow would make the track impassable and muffle what few sounds there were.

I stopped a couple of times to catch my breath. I walk about London and other cities a great deal, but that is easy walking and does not prepare one for such a steep climb. I wiped my face on my jacket sleeve and carried on.

And then, quite suddenly, I was out from between the trees and looking down the slope of a stony outcrop on to the monastery of Saint Mathieu des Etoiles.

The roofs were of dark grey shingle and the whole formed an enclosed rectangle with two single buildings on the short sides, one of which had a high bell tower. The long sides were each divided into two dozen identical units. There was a second, smaller rectangle of buildings to the north. The whole was set on the level and surrounded by several small fenced pastures, but beyond these the ground was sheer, climbing to several high peaks. The slopes were pine-forested. The sun came out for a moment, bathing the whole in a pleasant and tranquil light. The sky was blue above the peaks, though there were also skeins of cloud weaving between them. I heard the tinkle of a cowbell, of the sort that rings gently all summer through the Swiss Alps. A bee droned on a ragged purple plant at my feet. The rest was the most deep and intense silence.

I stood, getting my breath and bearings, the canvas bag slung across my shoulders, and for the first time that day I felt a slight lifting of the fear that had oppressed me. And I also recalled that somewhere in that compact group of ancient buildings below were the most extraordinary treasures, books, icons, pictures – who knew what else?

I shifted the bag on to my left shoulder and began to make my way carefully down the steep and rocky path towards the monastery.

꜔

I DO NOT know what I expected. The place was silent save for a single bell tolling as I approached the gate. It stopped and all I could hear were those faint natural sounds, the rain dripping off roofs and trees, the stream. But when the door in the great wooden gate was opened to me and I gave my name, I was greeted by a smiling, burly monk in a black hooded habit and a large cotton apron. He greeted me in English.

'You are welcome, Monsieur Snow. I am Frère Jean-Marc, the Guest Master. Please ...' – and he took my bag from me, lifting it as if it contained air and feathers.

He asked me where I had left my car and nodded approval as he led me across an inner courtyard towards a three-storey building.

Every sound had its own resonance in such a silent atmosphere. Our footsteps, separate and in rhythm, the monk's slight cough, another bell.

'You have come a long way to visit us.'

'Yes. I also came through a terrible storm just now.'

'Ah, mais oui, the rain, the rain. But our storms go as quickly as they come. It's the mountains.'

'The road is treacherous. I'm not used to such bends.'

He laughed. 'Well, you are here. You are welcome.'

We had climbed three flights of stone stairs and walked along a short corridor to the door which he now opened, standing aside to let me pass.

'Welcome,' he said again.

I felt real warmth in his greeting. Hospitality to strangers was an important part of the monastic rule, for all that these monks did not receive many.

I walked into the small, square room. The window opposite looked directly on to the pine-covered slopes and the jagged mountain peak. The sun was out, slanting towards us and lighting the deep, dark green of the trees, catching the whitewashed stone walls of the surrounding monastery buildings.

'Ah,' the Guest Master said, beaming, 'beautiful. But you should see it in the snow. That is a sight.'

'I imagine you have few guests in winter.'

'None, Monsieur. For some months we are impassable. Now, here … your bed. Table. Your chair. On here you see a letter from the Abbot to you, a letter also from Dom Martin, the Librarian. This list is our timetable. Here is a small map. But I will fetch you at the times you will meet. You are welcome to walk outside anywhere save the private cloister. You are welcome, most welcome, to attend any service in the chapel and I will take you in half an hour, to show you where this is, where you may sit, the dining room. But for now I will bring you refreshment in this room, so that you may get used to the place. You will meet the brothers also about the monastery, the brothers at work. Of course, please greet them. They are glad to welcome a guest. Now, I will leave you to become at home, and I will return with some food and drink.'

The room was peaceful. The sun moved round to shine on the white wall and the white cover of the iron-framed single bed. The window was open slightly. I could hear the distant sound of the cowbells.

For a moment, I thought that I would weep.

Instead, the walls seemed to shimmer and fold in upon themselves like a pack of cards and I fainted at Frère Jean-Marc's feet.

Eleven

I woke to find myself lying on the bed with the kindly and concerned face of the Guest Master looking down on me. There was another monk on my left side, holding my wrist to take the pulse, an older man with wrinkled, parchment-like skin and soft blue eyes.

'Now, Monsieur Snow, lie still, relax, You gave us a great shock. This is Dom Benoît, our Infirmarian. Il est médecin. His English is a little less than mine.'

I struggled to sit up but the old man restrained me gently. 'Un moment,' he said. 'You do not race away ...'

I lay back. Through the window I could see the mountain peak and a translucent blue sky. I felt strangely calm and at peace.

IN THE END, Dom Benoît seemed to decide that I was none the worse for my fainting attack and allowed me to sit up. There was a tray of food on the table by the window, with a carafe of water, and I went to it after both men had left, feeling suddenly hungry. The Guest Master had said that I should rest for the afternoon, sleep if possible, and that he would come back later to check up on me and, if the Infirmarian agreed, take me to my appointment with the Librarian.

I ate a bowl of thick vegetable soup that tasted strongly of celery, some creamy Brie-like cheese and fresh bread, a small salad and a bowl of cherries and grapes. The water must have come from a spring in the mountains – it had the unmistakable coolness and fresh taste that only such water has.

I felt perfectly well now, but slightly light-headed. I supposed that I had fainted in the aftermath of the morning's awful drive, though I do not remember ever passing out in my life before. I noticed that there was a faint redness on my upper arm where Dom Benoît had probably taken my blood pressure. I was being looked after with care.

As I ate I looked at the letters that had been left for me. The first, from the Librarian, suggested a meeting that evening, when he would be glad to show me both the First Folio and any other books I might like to see. I would also be welcome to visit the book bindery. The letter from the Abbot was brief, formal and courteous, simply bidding me welcome and hoping that he would be able to see me at some point during my stay.

The timetable, which had been typed out to give me an idea of how the monastic day and night were organised, was a formidable one. There was a daily mass, all the usual offices, the angelus and much time for private prayer and meditation. The monks ate together only once a day, in the evening, otherwise meals were taken in the solitude of their cells, or at their work.

There was a map of both the inside and the outside of the monastery, with a dotted red line, or cross, indicating areas to which I did not have access. But I was free to walk almost anywhere outside. I could go into the chapel, the refectory, the library and the communal areas of the cloisters. It seemed that I was also free to visit the kitchens and the carpentry shops and the cellars, the dairy and the cowsheds if I wished.

When I began to eat I had thought I would take a walk in the grounds near to the buildings as soon as I had finished the last mouthful. But I had barely begun to eat the fruit when a tiredness came over me that made my head swim and my limbs feel as heavy as if they had been filled with sawdust.

I opened the window more, so that the sweet air blew in from the mountain, with a breath of pine. Then I lay down and, to the gentle sound of the cowbells, I fell into the deepest sleep I have ever known.

↜

I WOKE INTO a soft mauve twilight. The stars had come out behind the mountain and there was a full moon. I lay still, enjoying the extraordinary silence. The morning's drive through the storm and the horror of almost running over the child seemed to belong to another time. I felt as if I had been in this small, whitewashed, peaceful room for weeks. After a few moments, I heard the bell sound somewhere in the monastery, calling the monks to more prayer, more solemn chant.

I got up cautiously but I was no longer in the least dizzy, though my limbs still felt heavy. I went to the window to breathe in the evening air. A fresh jug of water had been placed on the table and I drank a glass of it with as much relish as I had ever drunk a glass of fine wine.

I watched the sky darken and the stars grow brighter. I wondered if I could find my way outside. I felt like walking at least a little way, but as I was thinking of it I heard quick footsteps and the Guest Master tapped and came in, smiling. He was a man whose face seemed to be set in a permanent beam of welcome and good spirits.

'Ah, Monsieur Snow, bonsoir, bonsoir. It is good. I came in and each time …' He made a gesture of sleep, closing his eyes, with his hands to the side of his head.

'Thank you, yes. I slept like a newborn.'

'And so, you seem well again, but the Infirmarian will come again once more to be sure.'

'No, I'm fine. Please don't trouble the father again. Is it too late for my meeting with the Librarian?'

'Ah, I fear yes. But he will be pleased to meet with you tomorrow morning. I did not wake you. It was better.'

'I was wondering if I could take a short walk outside? I feel I need some fresh air.'

'Ah. Now, let me see. I have the office soon, but yes, come with me, come with me, take a little air – it is very mild. I will come to fetch you inside after the office and then it will be bringing your supper. We retire to bed early you see, and then tomorrow you will eat in the refectory with us, our guest. Please.' He held open the door for me and we went out of the room and down the corridor.

The stone staircase led into a long, cool cloister and as we walked down it I heard the sound of footsteps coming from all sides, soft, quick, pattering on the stone, and then the monks appeared, hoods up, heads bowed, arms folded within the wide sleeves of their habits.

But the Guest Master led me out of a door at the far end of the cloister and into a wide courtyard under the stars. He pointed to a door in the wall.

'There, please, walk out of there and into the cloister garden. You will find it so still and pleasant. I will return for you in twenty minutes. Tomorrow, you see, you will find it easy to make your own way about.'

He beamed and turned back, going quickly after the other monks towards the chapel, from where the bell continued to toll.

Twelve

I walked between the monastery buildings towards the cloister at the far end. No one was here save a scraggy little black and white cat which streaked away into the shadows on my approach. I looked with pleasure at the beauty of the pattern made by the line of arches and at the stones of the floor. There was no sound. The singing of the monks at their office was contained somewhere deep within the walls. At the end of the cloister, I stepped off the path and onto closely cut grass. I had found myself in the garden, though one without any flowerbeds or trees. I stopped. I was surrounded by cloisters on three sides, on the fourth by another building. There was moonlight enough to see by.

I wondered what kind of men came here to stay not for a few days' retreat or refreshment, but for life. Unusual men, it might seem. Yet the Guest Master was robust and energetic, a man you might meet anywhere.

I wondered how I would find the Librarian and the Abbot. And as I did so, I began to cross the grass. It was as I reached the centre of the large rectangular garden that I noticed the pool. It too was rectangular, with wide stone surrounds and set level with the ground. I wondered if there were fish living a cool mysterious life in its depths.

It was as I drew close to it and looked down that I felt the small hand holding mine. I thought my heart would stop. But this time the hand did not clutch mine and there was no sense that I was being pulled forward. It was, as on that first evening, merely a child's hand in mine.

I looked down into the still, dark water on which the moonlight rested and as I looked I saw. What I saw was so clear and so strange and so real that I could not doubt it then, as I have never doubted it since.

I saw the face of a child in the water. It was up-turned to look directly at me. There was no distortion from the water, it was not the moonlight playing tricks with the shadows. Everything was so still that there was not the slightest ripple to disturb the surface. It was not easy to guess at his age but he was perhaps three or four. He had a solemn and very beautiful face and the curls of his hair framed it. His eyes were wide open. It was not a dead face, this was a living, breathing child, though I saw no limbs or body, only the face. I looked into his eyes and he looked back into mine, and as we looked the grip of the small hand tightened. I could hardly breathe. The child's eyes had a particular expression. They were beseeching me, urging me. I closed my eyes. When I opened them, he was still there.

Now the small hand was tightening in mine and I felt the dreadful pull I had experienced before to throw myself forward into the water. I could not look at the child's face, because I knew that I would be unable to refuse what he wanted. His expression was one of such longing and need that I could never hold out against him. I closed my eyes, but then the pull of the hand became so strong that I was terrified of losing my balance. I felt both afraid and unwell, my heart pounding and my limbs weak so that, as I turned away from the pool, using every last ounce of determination, I stumbled and fell forward. As I did so, I reached my left hand across and tried to prise the grasp of the small fingers away, but there was nothing to take hold of, though the sensation of being held by them did not lessen.

'Leave me alone,' I said. 'Please go. Please go.' I heard myself speak but my voice sounded odd, a harsh whispered cry as I struggled to control my breathing.

The hand still tugged mine, urging me to stand up, urging me to do what it wanted me to do, go where it wanted me to go.

'Let me go!' I shouted, and my shout echoed out into the silent cloisters.

I heard an exclamation and a hurried movement towards me across the grass and Frère Jean-Marc was kneeling beside me, taking me by the shoulders and lifting me easily into a sitting position, tutting in a gentle voice and telling me to be calm.

After a moment, my breathing slowed and I stopped shaking. A slight breeze came from the mountain, cool on my face, smelling of the pine trees.

'Tell me,' the monk said, his face full of concern, 'tell me what is troubling to you. Tell me – what is it that is making you afraid?'

Thirteen

There could have been no place more calming to the senses or enriching to the spirit than the great library at the monastery of Saint Mathieu.

Sitting there the next day in that quiet and beautiful space, I counted myself one of the most fortunate men on earth, and nothing that had happened to me seemed to be more than the brush of a gnat against my skin.

The library was housed in a three-storey building separate from the rest, with a spiral stone staircase leading from the cloisters firstly into a simple reading room set with pale wooden desks, then up to the one holding, so the Librarian told me, all the sacred books and manuscripts, many of them in multiple copies.

But it was the topmost room, with its tall, narrow windows letting in lances of clear light and with a gallery all the way round, which took my breath away. If I could compare it to any other library I knew, it would be to the Bodleian's Duke Humfrey, that awe-inspiring space, but the monastery library was more spacious and without any claustrophobic feel.

At first, I had simply stood and gazed round me at the magnificence of the shelving, the solemnity of the huge collection, the order and symmetry of the great room. If the books had all been empty boxes it would still have been mightily impressive. There were slender stone pillars and recessed reading desks in the arched spaces between them.

The floor was of polished honey-coloured wood and there was a central row of tables. At the far end, behind a carved wooden screen, was the office of the Librarian. Along the opposite end were tall cupboards which contained, I was told, the most precious manuscripts in the collection.

The cupboards were not locked. When I noted this, the Librarian simply smiled. 'Mais pourquoi?'

Indeed. Where else in the world would so many rare and precious items be entirely safe from theft? The only reason they were kept out of sight was to protect them from damage.

THE LIBRARIAN HAD brought me book after wonderful book, simply for my delight – illuminated manuscripts, rare psalters, Bibles with magnificent bindings. He was an old man, rather bent, and he moved, as I had noticed all the monks moved, at a slow and measured pace, as if rush and hurry were not only wasteful of energy but unspiritual. Everything was accomplished but no one hurried. His English was almost flawless – he told me that he had spent five years studying at St John's College, Cambridge – and his interest and learning were wide, his pleasure in the library clear to see. He had a special dispensation to speak to me, but he did not waste a word any more than he wasted a movement.

I had slept well and dreamlessly after a late visit from the Infirmarian, who had given me what he described as 'un peu de somnifère gentil' – a dark green liquid in a medicine glass. He had checked me over and seemed satisfied that I was not physically ill. Frère Jean-Marc had brought my breakfast and explained that the Abbot had been spoken to and would like to see me at two o'clock but that he felt a visit to the library would be the best medicine. He was right.

'And now,' the Librarian, Dom Martin, had said,

coming towards the reading desk at which I was sitting in one of the alcoves.

From there, I could look into the body of the library, and the sunshine making a few lozenges of brightness on the wooden floor. The place smelled as all such places do, of paper and leather, polish and age and wisdom – a powerful intoxicant to anyone whose life is bound up, as mine had long been, with books.

'Here it is. Perhaps you have seen one of these before – there are over two hundred in the world, after all – but you will not have seen this particular one. I think you are about to have a wonderful surprise.' He smiled, his old face full of a sort of teasing delight as he held the book in his hands.

I had indeed seen a Shakespeare First Folio before. As he said, it is not particularly rare and I had looked closely at several both in England and abroad. I had also spent some time before coming to Saint Mathieu checking two existing Folios, so that I would be able to judge whether what I was to be shown was genuine. It was not impossible. The whereabouts of only a couple of hundred copies are known now, but the book would have had a printing of perhaps 750. Even if most of those did not survive, there was nothing to say several might not still remain, buried in some library – possibly, a library such as this one.

The book Dom Martin held in his outstretched hands was large. He laid it down with care on the desk before me but he did not wait for me to examine it. One of the innumerable bells was ringing, summoning him away to prayer. He walked out of the great room and I heard his footsteps going away down the stone staircase as the bell continued to toll. Two other monks, who had been at some quiet work, followed him and I was left alone to examine what I knew within a few moments to be, with precious little doubt, a very fine copy of the First Folio. That in itself was exciting enough, but in addition, on the title page, the book bore the signature of Ben Jonson. Of course I would need to check, but from memory I was sure the signature was right. So this, then, was his copy of Shakespeare that I held in my hands. It was a remarkable moment.

I spent some time turning the pages carefully, revelling in the book and hoping that I might manage to procure it for Sir Edgar Merriman. After a moment, I looked up and around that handsome room. I felt well. I felt quite calm. I also felt safe, as I no longer felt truly safe anywhere outside, for fear of what might happen and of feeling the small hand creeping into mine. I steered my attention quickly back to the book before me.

❧

I SPENT THE rest of the morning comfortably in the library before returning to my room at one o'clock, when the Guest Master brought my simple food. At two he returned to escort me to the Abbot. I had not left the building since the previous night, though I could see that it was a beautiful day and the bright sky and clear air ought to tempt me out. But whenever I so much as thought about venturing beyond the safety of the monastery walls, I felt a lurch of fear again.

❧

THE ABBOT WAS unlike the figure I had imagined. I had expected a tall, imposing, solemn, older man. He was small, with a neat-featured face, deepset eyes. He spoke good English, he listened carefully, he was rather expressionless but then his face would break into a warm, engaging smile. I warmed to him. I felt reassured by him and after ten minutes or so in his presence, I realised that he was a man with an unprepossessing exterior that concealed considerable human understanding and wisdom.

We talked business for a few moments in his tidy office, about the sale of the monastery's treasures and the Folio in particular, and I knew that things would probably be arranged smoothly. The deliberation about whether to sell anything at all had been long, careful and probably painful, but once the decision had been made, they would be quite pragmatic and arrange things efficiently. They had to ensure the upkeep and survival of the monastery for the future.

'Monsieur Snow, I would like you to feel you may stay with us here until you feel quite well again. We will look after you, of course. This is a very healing place.'

'I know. I feel that very much. And I am very grateful to you.'

He waited quietly, patiently, and as he waited I felt an urge to tell him, tell him everything that had happened, recount the strange events and my own terrors, ask him – for what? To believe me? To explain?

There was no sound in the room. I wondered what the monks were doing now and presumed they were in their own cells, praying, reading holy books, meditating. From far on the mountainside came the tinkle of the cowbells. I looked at the Abbot.

'I wonder,' I said, 'if I am going mad or being persecuted in some way. I only know that things keep happening to me which I do not understand. I have always been a healthy man and quite serene. Until — this began.'

His eyes were steady on my face, his hands still, resting on either side of his chair. His habit, with the hood back, lay in perfect folds, as if they had been painted by an old master. He did not urge me. I felt that he would accept whatever I chose to do — leave the room now, without saying more, or confide in him and ask for his counsel.

I began to talk. Perhaps I had not intended to tell him everything, even the details of my brother's own breakdown, but I found myself doing so. Once, he got up and poured me a glass of water from a carafe on the stone ledge. I drank it eagerly before continuing. The sunlight, which had been slanting across his desk, moved round and away. Twice the bell rang, but the Abbot took no notice of it, merely sat in his chair, his eyes on me, his expression full of concern, listening, listening.

I finished speaking and fell silent, suddenly drained of every gram of energy. I knew that when

I returned to the guest room I would sleep another of the deep, exhausted sleeps I had grown used to having in this place.

The Abbot sat thoughtfully for some moments as I leaned back, slightly dizzy but in some way washed clean and clear, as if I had confessed a catalogue of terrible sins to the priest.

At last I said, 'You think I am mad.'

He waved his hand dismissively. 'Mais non. I think terrible things have happened to you and you are profoundly affected by them. But what things and why? Can you tell me – nothing like this has ever happened in your life until the first visit to this house entirely by chance?'

'Absolutely nothing. Of that I'm quite certain.'

'And this hand? This hand of the child at first did not seem in any way upsetting?'

'No. It seemed very strange.'

'Bien sûr.'

'But it was not until later that I felt any hostility, any desire to do me harm. Real harm. To lead me into harm.'

'Into these pools. Into the water. Over the precipice into the lake of the gorge.'

'But why?' I cried out loudly. 'Why does this thing want to do me harm?'

'I think that either you can choose never to know that and simply pray that in time it will be tired of failure and abandon this quest. Or you can choose to find out, if that shall be possible, and so …'

'To lay the ghost.'

'Oui.'

'Do you believe this thing – child – whatever it is – do you believe it truly exists?'

'Spirits exist, bien sûr. Good exists. Evil exists. Perhaps the spirit of a child is disturbed and unhappy. Perhaps it has a need.' He shrugged. 'I do think you have suffered. I think you will do well to remain here and let us help you, refresh you.'

'But here of all places, surely, this should not have happened again? If I am not safe here …'

'You are entirely safe here. Do not doubt it. You will be given all the strength, all the protection of our Blessed Lord and his saints, and of our prayers for you. You are surrounded by strong walls of prayer, Monsieur Snow. Do not forget.'

'Thank you. I will try.'

'This evening, if you feel well and able, join us in the chapel for our night prayers. These give great peace, great power to combat the perils of the darkness. And if you decide to confront le fantôme, and your terrors, then you will also be under protection, under the shield of our prayers.'

'What do you honestly think I should do, Father?'

'Ah. For me, everything is the better when faced. You draw the sting. But you only can make this choice.'

He stood in one graceful, flowing movement of body and robes together and held up his right hand to make the sign of the cross over me, then led me towards the door. As I left, he stood watching me walk down the cloister and I glanced back, to see that his expression was grave. He had believed me. He had listened attentively and dismissed nothing, nor tried to explain any of it away. For that I was deeply grateful.

I RETURNED TO my room and slept, but when I woke I longed for outside air and found my way, with only a couple of wrong turnings down stone corridors, to the courtyard. This time, I walked in the opposite direction from the one I had taken the previous night and went instead through the gate in the wall to the main entrance and, from there, headed towards the pine-covered slopes and a narrow path that climbed steeply and would, I was sure, eventually lead to the top of one of the peaks. I am no mountaineer. I walked for perhaps twenty minutes along the narrow path that wound between the great, dark trees. The ground was soft with a carpet of pine needles, my feet made no sound and when I looked up I could see violet-blue patches of sky far above the treetops. I came to a clearing where two or three trees had been felled and were lying on the ground. I sat down. There was no birdsong, no animal movement, but tiny spiders and other insects scurried about on the logs and at my feet. I realised that I was waiting. I even held out my hand.

One of the small spiders ran across it. Nothing more.

I MADE MY way carefully back down the path. But when I went through the gate I heard voices coming not from inside the monastery but from somewhere beyond the outer courtyard. I found my way through the cloisters until I approached the inner garden. A group of about a dozen of the monks were standing around the pool. One held a thurible which he was swinging gently, sending soft clouds of incense drift-ing across the surface of the water. Another carried a cross. The rest were singing a plainchant, holding their books in front of them, heads slightly bowed. I stood still until the singing died away and then saw the Abbot lift his hand and give a final blessing while making the sign of the cross. I realised that the pool in which I had seen the upturned face of the child and towards which I had been so urgently drawn was being blessed, made holy. Made safe.

I was glad of it. But as I slipped back through the cloisters, I knew that the Abbot's precaution had not been necessary, for it was not the monks who were in danger, or indeed any other person who might visit this quiet and holy place. Whatever it was that had come here had come because of me. When I left, it would leave too. Leave with me.

Fourteen

Four Ragged Staff Lane
Oxford OX2 1ZZ

Adam,
Terrific news. Well done! I was sure you and the monks would see eye to eye and am delighted you confirmed that it was indeed a First Folio and managed to secure it. Lucky client.

Come to Oxford again soon.

Best,
Fergus

Ravenhead
Ditchforth
West Sussex

Dear Mr Snow

We are greatly looking forward to seeing you here on Wednesday next, to dine and sleep and tell us about your visit to France. My husband is on tenterhooks.

Meanwhile, having more time on my hands as I grow old than perhaps I should, I have been delving a little into the story of the White House and have turned up one or two snippets of information which can perhaps be pieced together. But it may no longer be of the slightest interest to you and of course you must tell me if that is the case.

We will expect you somewhere between five and six o'clock.

With every good wish
Alice Merriman

Hello. This is Adam Snow. I am sorry I am not available. Please leave me a message and I will return your call.

It's Hugo. Not sure if you're back. I've been thinking about what you told me when you came up here last time. I just wanted to say I'm sure it's nothing. Maybe you had a virus. You know, people get depression after flu, that sort of stuff. So, if you're worried about it, well, don't be. I'm sure it was nothing. OK, that's it. Give us a call some time.

Fifteen

Of course I had to return. As soon as I had arranged to go down and see Sir Edgar Merriman about the Folio, I became aware of the sensation. It was like a magnetic pull upon my whole being. It was there when I slept and when I woke, it was there at the back of my mind all day and it was there even within my dreams. I could not have resisted whatever force it was and I did not try. I was afraid of it and I think I knew now that the best, the only thing to do if I was to retain my sanity was to obey. I hoped that the monks were continuing to pray for my protection.

This time I did not get lost. This time I did not come upon it by chance. This time I had marked my journey out on a map a couple of days before and gone carefully over the last few miles, so that I knew exactly where I was going and how long it would take me from when I left the A road. This time I drove slowly down the lane, between the high banks, the elephantine tree trunks pressing in on me in the gloom, and I was aware of everything as if I had taken some mind-expanding drug, so clearly did I see it all, so vivid the detail of every last tree root and clump of earth and overhanging branch seem.

It was a tranquil day but with a cloudy sky. Earlier there had been a couple of showers and by the time I got out of the car in the clearing the air was humid and still.

I had come prepared. I had bought a pair of wire cutters and some secateurs. I was not going to let undergrowth or fences keep me out.

What would I find? I did not know and I tried not to give my imagination any rein. I would obey the insistent, silent voice that told me I must go back and once there I would see. I would see.

EVERYTHING SEEMED AS before. I stood for a moment beside the car and then went to the gate and pushed it open, feeling it scrape along the ground just as on my previous visit, and walked towards the old ticket booth. The notice still hung there, the grille was still down. I stood and waited for a moment. In my left hand I carried the cutters, my right held nothing. But after several minutes nothing had happened. My hand remained empty. In a gesture that was half deliberate, half a reflex, I curled my fingers. There was no response.

❧

THE AIR WAS heavy, the bushes on either side lush, the leaves of some ancient laurel glistening with moisture from the earlier rain. I had put on wellington boots, so that I could push my way through the long grass without inconvenience.

I came out into the clearing. There was the house. The White House. Empty. Half derelict, the glass broken in one or two of the windows. The stones of the courtyard in front of it were thick with pads of velvety moss.

I turned away. To the side was another low wooden gate. It had an old padlock and rusty chain across it and both gleamed with moisture. But the padlock hung open and the gate was so rotten it gave at once to my hand and I went through. Ahead of me was a path leading between some ancient high yew hedges. I followed it. I could see quite well because although the sky was overcast it was barely half past five and there was plenty of light left. The path led straight. At the end, an archway was cut into the hedge and although ivy trailed down over it, the way was clear and I had no need of the cutters I had brought. I went through and down four steps made of brick and set in a semi-circle, then found that I had come out into what had clearly once been a huge lawn with a high wall at the far end and the thickly overgrown remains of wide flower borders. There were fruit trees, gnarled and pitted old apples and pears, forming a sort of avenue – I know there are proper gardening terms for these things. On the far side of the lawn, whose grass was so high that it came over the tops of my boots and was mixed with nettles and huge vicious thistles, there ran yet another tall yew hedge in which was another arch. I turned round. To one side a path led diagonally towards woodland. I went in the opposite direction, to an open gate in a high wall. On the other side of it I found what seemed to have been an area of patterned beds set formally between old gravel paths. I remembered pictures of

Elizabethan knot gardens. There were small trees planted in the centre of each bed, though most of them looked dead. I leaned over and picked a wiry stem from a bush beside me, breaking it between my fingers. It was lavender.

Every so often, I paused and waited. But there was nothing. Nothing stirred and no birds sang.

ↄ

IT WAS A SAD place, but I did not feel uneasy or afraid in any way, there seemed to be nothing odd about this abandoned garden. I felt melancholy. It had once been a place of colour and beauty, full of growth and variety – full of people. I looked around me, trying to imagine them strolling about, bending over to look more closely at a flower, admiring, enjoying, in pairs or small groups.

Now there was no one and nature was taking everything back to itself. In a few more years would there be anything left to say there had been a garden here at all?

The silence was extraordinary, the same sort of silence I had experienced in the grounds of the monastery. But here there were no gentle cowbells reassuring me from the near distance. I wondered which way to go. I had come because I had had no choice. But what next?

As if in reply, the small hand crept into mine and held it fast and I felt myself pulled forward through the long grass towards the far hedge.

❦

THE SOFT SWISHING sound my boots made as I walked broke the oppressive stillness. Once I thought I heard something else, just behind me, and swung round. There was nothing. Perhaps a rabbit or a stray cat was following – I was going to say 'us', for that was unmistakably how I felt now. There were two of us.

I reached the far side and the arch in the high dark yew and stopped just inside it. Looking ahead, I could see that I was about to enter another garden, a sunken garden that was approached down the flight of a dozen steps at my feet, semicircular again and broken here and there, with weeds growing between the cracks. On the far side stood a vast cedar tree. A very overgrown gravel path ran all the way round. It was not a large enclosure and the surrounding yew hedge closed in like high, dark walls. Because of these and the trees on the other side, less light came in here than into the wide open space I had just left, and so the grass in the centre had not grown wild but was still short, something like a lawn, though spoiled by yellowish weed and with bald patches here and there, where the earth or stones showed through, like the skull through an old person's thinning hair.

I did not want to step down into it. I felt that if I did I would be suffocated between these dark hedges. But the small hand was holding mine tightly and trying with everything in its power to get me to move.

And then, as I looked down, I noticed something else. In the centre was a strange circle, like a fairy ring. I could only just make it out, for it seemed to be marked from nothing in particular – a darker line of grass perhaps, or small stones concealed below the surface. I stared at it and it seemed not to be there.

The grey clouds above me parted for a moment and a dilute and watery sun struggled through for a moment and in that moment the circle appeared quite clearly against a fleeting brightness.

꙳

THE SMALL HAND was grasping mine in

desperation now. It was as if someone was in danger of falling over the edge of a cliff and clutching at me for dear life, but at the same time it was trying to pull me over with it. If it fell it would make sure that I would fall too. It was exactly the same as it had been on the edge of the precipice in the Vercors, except that that had been real. Here there was no cliff, merely a few steps. I still did not want to go down, but I could no longer resist the strength of the hand.

'All right,' I said aloud, my voice sounding strange in that desolate place. 'All right. I'll do what you want.'

I went, being careful with my footing on the loose and cracked stones, until I was standing in the sunken garden, on the same level as the half-visible circle. But at that moment the sun went in and a sudden rush of wind blew, shifting the heavy branches of the great tree on the far side before it died away at once, leaving an eerie and total stillness.

'What are you doing here?'

The sound of the voice was like a shot in the back. I have never felt such a split second of absolute shock and terror.

'The garden is no longer open to the public.'

I turned.

SHE WAS STANDING at the top of the steps inside the archway, looking down, staring at me out of a face devoid of expression, and yet she gave off an air of hostility to me, of threat. She was old, though I could not guess, as one often can, exactly how old, but her face was a mesh of fine wrinkles and those do not come at sixty. Her hair was very thin and scraped back into some sort of comb and she seemed to be bundled into layers of old clothes, random skirts and cardigans and an ancient bone-coloured mackintosh, like a bag lady who preyed upon the rubbish sacks at the kerbside.

I stammered an apology, said I had not realised anyone would be there, thought the place was derelict ... I stumbled over my words because she had startled me and I felt somehow disorientated, which was perhaps because I was standing on a lower level, almost as if I were at her feet.

'Won't you come to the house?'

I stared at her.

'There is nothing here now. The garden has gone. But if you would like to see it as it was I would be glad to show you the pictures.'

'As it was?'

But she was turning away, a small, wild figure in her bundled clothing, the wisps of ancient grey hair escaping at the back of her neck like skeins of cloud.

'Come to the house …' Her voice faded away as she disappeared back into the tangled grass and clumps of weed that was the garden on the other side.

For a moment I did not move. I could not move. I looked down at my feet, to where I had seen the strange circle in the ground, but it was not there now. It had been some optical illusion, then, a trick of the light. In any case, I had no idea what I had thought it represented – perhaps the foundations of an old building, a summer house, a gazebo? I stepped forward and scraped about with my foot. There was nothing. I tried to remember the stories we had learned as children about fairy rings. Then I turned away. Somewhere beyond the arch, she would be waiting for me. 'Come to the house.'

Half of me was curious, wanting to know who she was and what I would find in a house I had thought was abandoned and semi-derelict. But I was afraid too. I thought I might dive back through the under-growth until I reached the gate and the drive, the safety of my car, ignore the old woman. Run away.

It was my choice.

I waded my way through the undergrowth beneath the gathering sky. It was airless and very still. The silence seemed palpable, like the silence that draws in around one before a storm.

It was only as I reached the path that led out of the gardens between overgrown shrubs and trees towards the gate that I realised I was alone. The old woman had vanished and the small hand was no longer grasping mine.

Sixteen

The key was in my trouser pocket. I had only to open the car doors, throw in the tools and get away from that place, but as I went I glanced quickly back over my shoulder at the house. The door was standing wide open where I was certain that it had previously been shut fast. I hesitated. I wanted to turn and head for the car but I was transfixed by sight of the door, sure that the old woman must have opened it because she was expecting me to enter, was waiting for me now somewhere inside.

'Are you there?' she called.

So I had no choice after all. I dropped the secateurs and cutters on the ground and went slowly towards the house, looking up as I did so at the windows whose frames were rotten, at the paint that was faded and peeled almost away, at the window-panes which were filthy and broken here and there, and in a couple of the rooms actually boarded over. Surely no one could possibly live here. Surely this place was, as I had seen it at first, ruined and deserted.

I walked up the steps and hesitated at the open door. I could see nothing inside the house, no light, no movement.

'Hello?' My voice echoed down the dark corridor ahead.

There was no reply. No one was here. The wind had blown the door open. Yet the old woman had been in the garden. I had seen her and she had spoken to me. Then I heard a sound, perhaps that of a voice. I took a step inside.

It was several moments before my eyes grew used to the darkness, but then I saw that I was standing in a hall and that a passageway led off to my right. I saw a glimmer of light at the far end. Then the voice again.

The house smelled of rot and mould and must. This could not possibly still be a home. It must not have been inhabited for decades. I put out my hand to touch the wall and then guide myself along the passage, though I was sure that I was being foolish and told myself to go back. I had only just regained my senses and a measure of calm since the awful things that had happened: in Oxford, in the mountains of the Vercors and the garden of the monastery. I was certain that those things were somehow connected with this house, and my first visit here, with the first time I had felt the small hand take hold of mine. Was I mad? I should not have come back and I certainly should not be going any further now.

But I was powerless to stop. I could not go back. I had to know.

Keeping my hand to the wall, which was cold and crumbled to the touch of my fingers here and there, I made my way with great caution down the passage in the direction of what, after a few yards, I thought was the light of candles.

'Please come in.'

IT TOOK ME a few seconds to orientate myself within one of the weirdest rooms I had ever entered. The wavering tallow light came not from candles after all, but from a couple of ancient paraffin lamps which gave off a strong smell. There was even a little daylight in the room too, filtering in through

French windows at the back, but the glass was filthy, the creeper and overhanging greenery outside obscured much of it and it was impossible to tell if the sky was thundery and dark or whether it was simply occluded by the dirt.

It was a large room but whole recesses of it were in shadow and seemed to be full of furniture swathed in sheeting. Otherwise, it was as if I had entered the room in which the boy Pip had encountered Miss Havisham.

In one corner was a couch which seemed to be made up as a bed with a pile of cushions and an ancient quilt thrown over it. There was a wicker chair facing the French windows and a dresser with what must once have been a fine set of candelabra and rows of rather beautiful china, but the silver was tarnished and stained, the china and the dresser surface covered in layers of dust.

She was sitting at a large round table in the centre of the room, on which one of the lamps stood, the old mackintosh hanging on her chair-back but the rest of her still huddled in the mess of ragged old clothes. Her scalp looked yellow in the oily light, which shone through the frail little pile of hair on top of her head.

'I must apologise,' she said. 'There are so few

visitors now. People still remember the garden, you know, and occasionally they come here, but not many. It is all a long time ago. Look out there.'

I followed her gaze, beyond the dirty windows to where I could make out a veranda, with swags of wisteria hanging down in uneven curtains, and another wicker chair.

'I can see the garden better from there. Won't you sit down?'

I hesitated. She leaned over and swept a pile of all manner of rubbish, including old newspapers, cardboard and bits of cloth, off a chair beside her.

'I will show you the pictures first,' she said. 'Then we can go round the garden.'

I had had no idea that anyone could possibly be living here and now I had found her I could not imagine how she did indeed 'live', how she ate and if she ever left the place. She was clearly half mad, an ancient woman living in some realm of the past. I wondered if she belonged here, if she had been a housekeeper, or had just come upon it and broken in, a squatter among the debris and decay.

She looked up at me. Her eyes were watery and pale, like the eyes of most very old people, but there was something about the look in them that unnerved me. Her skin was powdery and paper-thin, her nose a bony hook. It was impossible to guess her age. And yet there was a strange beauty about her, a decaying, desiccated beauty, but it held my gaze for all that. She seemed to belong with those dried and faded flowers people used to press between pages, or with a bowl of old potpourri that exudes a faint, sweet, ghostly scent when it is disturbed. Yet when she spoke again her voice was clear and sharp, with an elegant pronunciation. Nothing about her added up.

'I think you've visited the garden before Mr ...'

'No. I got lost down the lane leading to the house one evening a few months ago. I'd never heard of the garden. And my name is Snow.'

She was looking at me with an odd, quizzical half-smile.

'Do please sit down. I said I would show you the albums. People sometimes come for that, you know, as well as those who expect the garden still to be open and everything just as it was.' She looked up at me. 'But nothing is ever just as it was, is it, Mr Snow?'

'I don't think I caught your name.'

'I presumed you knew.' She went on looking at me for a second or two, before pulling a large leather-bound album towards her from several on the table. The light in the room was eerie, a strange mixture of the flickering oil lamp and the grey evening seeping in from outside, filtered through the overhanging creeper.

'You really cannot look at these standing up. But perhaps I can get you something? It is rather too late for tea. I could offer you sherry.'

'Thank you. No. I really have to leave, I'm afraid. I'm on my way to stay with friends – I still have some miles to drive. I should have left …'

I heard myself babbling on. She sat quite still, her hand on the album, as if waiting patiently for my voice to splutter and die before continuing.

For a second the room was absolutely silent and we two frozen in it, neither of us speaking, neither moving, and as if something odd had happened to time.

I knew that I could not leave. Something was keeping me here, partly but not entirely against my will, and I was calmly sure that if I tried to go I would be detained, either by the old woman's voice or by the small hand, which for the moment at least was not resting in mine. But if I tried to escape, it would be there, gripping tightly, holding me back.

I pulled out a chair and sat down, a little apart from her, at the dark oak table, whose surface was smeared with layers of dirt and dust.

She glanced at me and I saw it again, the strange

beauty shining through age and decay, yellowing teeth and desiccated skin and dry wisps of old hair.

'This was the house when I first found it. And the garden. Not very good photographs. Little box cameras.'

She shook her head and turned the page.

'The wilderness,' she said, looking down. 'That's what the children said when we first came here. I re-member so well – Margaret rushing round the side of the house and looking at it – the huge trees, weeds taller than she was, rhododendrons ...' She lifted her hand above her head. 'She stopped there. Look, just there. Michael came racing after her and they stood together and she shouted, "It's our wilderness!"'

She rested her hand on the photograph and was silent for a moment. I could see the pictures, tanned with age and rather small. But it was all familiar, because it was all the same as today. The wilderness had grown back, the house was as dilapidated as it had been all those years ago. All those years? How many? How old was she?

'You!' I said suddenly. 'You are Denisa Parsons. It was your garden.'

'Of course,' she said dismissively. 'Who did you think I was?'

My head swam suddenly and the table seemed to

pitch forward in front of me. I reached out my hand to grab hold of it.

She was smiling vaguely down at the album and now she began to turn the pages one after the other, making an occasional remark. 'The builders ... look ... digging out the ground ... trees coming down ... light ... so much light suddenly.'

The flicking of the pages confused me. I felt nauseated. The smell of the paraffin was sickening, the room fetid. There was another smell. I supposed it was accumulated dirt and decay.

'I'm trying to find it.' Flick. Flick. 'Margaret never forgave me. Nor Michael, but Michael was more stoical, I suppose. And then of course he went away. But Margaret. It was hate. Bitter hate. You see –' she rested her hand on the table and stared down, as if reading something there – 'I sent them away to boarding school. When we first came here, after Arthur died, it never occurred to me that I would want them out of the way. He had left me the money, enough to buy somewhere else, and I had never liked the suburbs. But when we came here something happened. I had to do it, you see, I had to pull it all down and make something magnificent of my own. And they were in the way.'

She turned a page, then another.

'Here it is, you see. Here it all is. The past is here. Look … the Queen came. Here she is. There were pieces in all the newspapers. Look.'

But I could not look, for she was turning the pages too quickly, and when she had got to the end of the book, she reached for another.

'I have to go,' I said. 'I have to be somewhere else.'

She ignored me.

I stood up and pushed back my chair. The room seemed to be closing in on us, shrinking to the small area round the table, lit by the oily lamplight.

I almost pitched forward. I felt nauseous and dizzy.

And then she let out an odd laugh. 'Here,' she said. 'This one. Look here.'

She turned the album round so that I could see it. There were four photographs on the left and two on the right-hand side, all of them cut from newspapers and somewhat faded.

They seemed to be of various parts of the White House garden as it had been – the yew hedge was visible in one, a series of interlinked rose arches in another. There were groups of visitors strolling across a lawn. The one she pointed to seemed to be of a broad terrace on which benches were placed in front of a stone balustrade. Several large urns were spilling over with flowers. It was just possible to see steps leading down, presumably to a lower level and another part of the garden.

She was not pointing to the book. She was sitting back in her chair and seemed to be looking into some far distance, almost unaware of where she was or of my presence. She was so totally still that I wondered for a second if she was still breathing.

And then, because now it was what I had to do, I could not turn my eyes away, I looked down at the page of photographs, and then, bending my head to see it more closely, to the one on the right at which she had pointed. There was a caption – I do not remember what it read but it was of no consequence, perhaps 'A sunny afternoon' or 'Visitors enjoying the garden'. I saw that the cutting was from a magazine and that it seemed to be part of a longer feature, with several double columns and another smaller picture. But it was not the writing, it was not the headline at which I was staring.

The black-and-white photograph of the terrace showed a couple beside one of the benches and seated on the bench in a row were some children. Three boys. Neat, open-necked white shirts. Grey trousers. White socks. Sandals. One wore a sleeveless pullover knitted in what looked like Fair Isle.

I looked at it more closely and, as I did so, I had a strange feeling of familiarity, as if I knew the pullover. And then I realised that it was not only the pullover which was familiar. I knew the boy. I knew him because he was myself, aged perhaps five years old. I remembered the pullover because it had been mine. I could see the colours: fawn, pale blue, brown.

I was the boy in the pullover and the one sitting next to me was my brother, Hugo.

But who the other boy was, the boy who sat at the end of our row and who was younger than either of us, I had no idea. I did not remember him.

'Come outside,' she was saying now. 'Let me show you.'

Yes. I needed to be outside, to be anywhere in the fresh air and away from the house and that room with its smell, and the yellowing light. I followed her, thinking that, whatever happened, I had the key to the car in my pocket, I could get in and go within a few moments. But she was not leaving the room by the open door into the dark corridor, she had gone across to the French windows and turned the key. Yet surely these glass doors could not have been opened for years. The creeper was twined thick as rope around the joints and hinges.

They opened easily, as such a door would in a

dream, and she brushed aside the heavy curtain of greenery as if it were so many overhanging cobwebs and I stepped out after her on to the wide veranda. It was twilight but the sky had cleared of the earlier, heavy cloud.

I remember that she turned her head and that she looked at me as I stood behind her. I remember her expression. I remember her eyes. I remember the way the old clothes she wore bunched up under the ancient mac when we had been inside the house.

I remember those things and I have clung on to the memory because it is – was – real, I saw those things, I was there. I could feel the evening air on my face. This was not a dream.

Yet everything that happened next had a quite different quality. It was real, it was happening, I was there. Yet it was not. I was not.

I despair. I am confused. I do not know how to describe what I felt, though in part the simple word 'unwell' would suffice. My legs were unsteady, my heart raced and I had seconds of dizziness followed by a sudden small jolt, like an electric shock, as if I had somehow come back into myself.

AS WE LEFT the shadow of the house and went down the stone steps, the evening seemed to retreat – the sun was still out after all and the air was less cold. I supposed heavy clouds had made it seem later and darker and now those were clearing, giving us a soft and slightly pearlescent end to the day.

Denisa Parsons stayed a few paces ahead of me and, as we walked, I saw that we must have come out on to a different side of the garden, one which I had not seen before and not even guessed about, a part that was still carefully tended – still a garden and not a jungle. The grass was mown, the paths were gravelled and without weeds and a wide border against a high stone wall still flowered with late roses among the green shrubs. I looked around, trying to get my bearings. I still felt unsteady. A squirrel sprang from branch to branch of a huge cedar tree to my right, making me start, but the old woman did not seem to notice, she simply walked on, and her walk was quite steady and purposeful, not faltering or cautious as I would have expected.

'I had no idea you kept up some of the garden like this,' I said. 'I thought it had all gone back to nature. You must have plenty of help.'

She did not reply, only went on, a few steps ahead of me, neither turning her head again nor giving any sign that she had registered my words. We went down a gravel path which was in heavy shade, towards a yew hedge I thought looked familiar — but all high, dark green hedges look alike to me and there was nothing to distinguish it. The grass was mown short but there were no more flowerbeds and, as we continued on the same, rather monotonous way, I thought that maintenance must probably be done by some outside contractor who came in once a week to mow and trim hedges. A couple of times a year he might spray the gravel to get rid of weeds. What else was there to do?

The shade was reaching across the grass like fingers grasping at the last of the sunlight. And then she turned.

We had reached the arch in the yew hedge and were at the top of the flight of stone steps, looking down to where I had seen the sunken garden, over-grown and wild, its stone paths broken and weed-infested. Below me had been the strange circle, like a shading in the grass, which had been there and then not there, an optical illusion, perhaps caused by a cloud moving in front of the sun.

But what I saw ahead was not a wilderness. It

certainly seemed to be the same sunken garden, reminding me of somewhere Italian I must once have visited, but it was immaculately ordered, with low hedges outlining squares and rectangles that contained beds of what I recognised as herbs, very regularly arranged. There were raked gravel paths and, on the far side, another flight of steps leading up to some sort of small stone temple.

And then I glanced down. At my feet was not some shadowy outline, like a great fairy-ring, but a pool, a still, dark pool set flat into the grass and with a stone rim, and I saw that, as this was a very formal garden of careful symmetry, its exact counterpart was on the opposite side. In between them stood a stone circle on which was an elaborate sundial painted in enamelled gold and blue.

But it was the pool into which I stared now, the pool with its few thick, motionless, flowerless lily pads and its slow, silent fish moving about heavily under the surface of the water.

I turned to Denisa Parsons to ask for an explanation, but as I did so two things happened very quickly.

The small hand had crept into mine and begun to pull me forward with a tremendous, terrifying strength and, as it did so, a voice spoke my name. It was a real voice, and I seemed to know whose voice it was, yet it sounded different, distorted in some way.

It was whispering my name over and over again and the whisper grew louder and clearer and more urgent. On every previous occasion, whoever the owner of the small hand might be, that person had always been completely silent. I had never heard the faintest whisper on the air. But now I heard something quite clearly.

'Adam!' it said. 'Adam. Adam. Adam.' Then silence, and my name again, the cry growing a little louder and more urgent. 'Adam. Adam.' At the same time, the small hand was pulling me so hard I lost my balance and half fell down the steps, and went stumbling after it, or with it, as it dragged me towards the pool.

I closed my eyes, fearful of what was there, what I knew that I should see, as I had seen it in the pool at the monastery.

'Here. Here. Here.'

I flung my right arm up into the air to shake off the grip of the small hand and, as I did so, looked towards the archway in some sort of desperate plea to the old woman to help me.

She was not there. The arch in the hedge was

hollow, with only darkness, like a blank window, behind.

✎

I DO NOT know if I cried out, I do not remember if the hand still clung to mine. I do not know anything, other than that the voice was still in my ears but wavering and becoming fainter and slightly distorted as the world tumbled in upon me and I felt myself fall, and not onto the hard ground but into a bottomless, swirling, dark vortex that had opened up at my feet.

Seventeen

I am sure that for a few minutes I must have been unconscious, before I felt myself surfacing, as if I had been diving in deep water and was slowly coming to the light and air. But the air felt close and damp and there was very little light. How long had I been at the house? I had gone there in daylight, now it was almost dark.

I was lying on the ground. I reached out my hand and felt cold stone and something rough. Gravel. Gradually, my head cleared and I found that I could sit up. It took me several minutes to remember where I was. The garden was dark, but when my eyes adjusted to it I could see a little.

I seemed to be unhurt, although I was dazed.

Had I fainted? Had I tripped and fallen and perhaps knocked myself out? No, because I would surely have felt pain somewhere and there was none.

I was alone. The garden was still. The bushes and trees around me did not rustle or stir. No bird called.

I waited until fragments of recollection floated nearer to me and began to form clearer shapes in my mind. The old woman in the strange bundled clothing. The room in which she lived in squalor, deep in the near-derelict house. Their smell. The wavering sound of her voice. The garden.

That part of the garden she had led me into which was not overgrown and neglected, but mown and tidy, with lawn and trees, shrubs and flowerbeds, arches in the high hedge leading down neat flights of steps to ...

I got carefully to my feet.

I saw the dark gleaming surface of the pool, the flat stone ledge that ran round it.

Golden fish gliding beneath the surface.

A bench.

Had there been a bench?

Bench. Bench.

My legs gave way beneath me again and I felt a wave of nausea. Bile rose into my mouth and I retched onto the cold ground.

AND THEN I heard something, some ordinary and reassuringly familiar sound. The sound of a car. I wiped my mouth on the back of my hand.

I could not get up again and for a while everything was dark and silent, but after a moment I saw a light flash somewhere, dip away, flash again, and a few moments later heard something else, the sound of someone pushing through the undergrowth. And calling out.

'Mr Snow? Mr Snow?'

I tried to reply but made only an odd, strangled sound in my throat.

The light sliced across the grass behind me.

'Mr Snow?'

I did not recognise the voice.

'Are you there? Mr Snow?'

And then someone almost tripped over me and the beam of a large torch was shining into my face and the man was bending down to me, murmuring with surprise and concern.

I closed my eyes in overwhelming relief.

Eighteen

I lay awake for a long time that night. I had been given a stiff whisky on arriving at the Merrimans' and then encouraged to have a hot bath. Lady Merriman was anxious for me to stay in bed and be given supper on a tray, but I wanted to get back to normality by eating with them, talking, giving all my news about the First Folio, so that I would not have to spend time alone going over what had – or had not – happened. I was quickly restored by the good malt and deep hot water and felt no after-effects of my having – what? Tripped and fallen, knocking myself out? Fainted? I had no idea and preferred not to speculate, but certainly I was not injured in any way, apart from having a sore bruise on my elbow where it had hit the ground under my weight.

Lady Merriman said little but I knew that her sharp blue eyes missed nothing and that, in spite of her usual quiet reserve, she was the one who had raised the alarm and who had guessed where I might be found when I failed to arrive at the house.

She told me that the police had been called first, but that there were no reports of road accidents.

'Then I had a sixth sense, you know,' she said. 'And that has never let me down. I knew you were there. I hope you don't think that weird in any way, Mr Snow. I am not a witch. But people don't always like it if you mention things of this sort. I have learned to stay silent.'

'I am very grateful for your sixth sense,' I said. 'Nor do I find it in the least weird. A lot of people have a slightly telepathic side to them … I am inclined to think it fairly normal. My mother often knew when a letter would arrive from someone, even if she was not expecting it and indeed hadn't heard from that person for years.'

'My husband is sceptical, but you know, after all this time even he has learned not to argue with my instincts. It doesn't often happen but when it does …'

'Well, thank God it did today. I might have been

lying there all night. I probably tripped on some of that wretched broken pathway and bumped my head.'

She said nothing.

THE EVENING WAS enjoyable because of my host's obvious delight in hearing that he was very likely to be the owner of a First Folio within the next few weeks. How it was to be transported to him was a minor problem, though I warned that it would have to be done before Christmas or he would not get the volume until the spring – the monastery is usually snowed in between early January and March. He suggested the best and safest way was for me to travel to collect it – I knew the place, I would be trusted and naturally both the book and I would be heavily insured. But everything in me recoiled at the idea of returning to Saint Mathieu, not because of the responsibility of carrying the book but because I felt that anything might happen in that place, as it already had happened, and I did not trust that I could travel there and back without the return of something that would once again cause me to experience terror. Because I realised that, other than the slight mishap today, I had never actually come to any real harm. What I had experienced was the extremes of fear and they were dreadful enough for me to want to avoid them at all cost. I could not speak of any of this. I simply said that I felt a professional firm used to transporting items of great value would be better bringing the Folio to England. I knew one which was entirely reliable, if costly, and Sir Edgar agreed to let me suggest the arrangement to the monastery once the deal had been finally agreed and the money paid.

IT WAS A CLOSE, thundery end to the day. The doors were open on to the garden and we could see the odd flash of lightning over the sea in the distance. Sir Edgar had brought up a bottle of fine old brandy to celebrate his latest acquisition and we talked on until late. Lady Alice glanced at me occasionally and I sensed that she was concerned, but she said nothing more until we were going upstairs just after midnight.

'Mr Snow, I have been rummaging about and finding some more things about the White House and its garden, if you are still interested. I have set them out in the small study for you – do look at them tomorrow if you would like to. But perhaps you've had enough of all that after your visit there today. I spoke to a friend who lives not far away and she said the place has been quite derelict and shut up for some years now. Everyone wonders why no one has bought it or had it restored. It seems terrible for it to be allowed to fall to bits like that. Anyway, I wish you a good rest and you know where the small study is if you do want to have a look through what I found.'

I had bidden her goodnight and closed my door, walked to the window and was standing looking out into the darkness and listening to the thunder, which was now rolling inland towards the house, before the meaning of what Lady Alice had said hit me.

It was hopeless then to try and sleep. I read for a while but the words slid off the surface of my mind. I opened the window. It was raining slightly and the air was heavy, but there was the chill of autumn on it.

I put on my dressing gown, but as I moved towards the door the bedside lamp went out. There was a small torch lantern beside it for just this eventuality and by the light of it I made my way quietly across the wide landing and down the passage that led to the small study. My torch threw its beam onto the wood panelling and the pictures on the walls beside me, mainly rather heavy oils of ancient castles and sporting men. Sir Edgar had a very fine collection of eighteenth-century watercolours in the house but up here nothing was of much beauty or interest. Once or twice my torch beam slipped over the eyes of a man or a dog, once over a set of huge teeth on a magnificently rearing stallion and the eyes and the teeth gleamed in the light. The thunder cracked almost overhead and lightning sizzled down the sky.

I found a number of magazines and newspapers laid out on the round table, opened at articles about the White House and its garden, but there were none of the photographs I had been given a glimpse of earlier, though I looked closely for the picture of myself, as a small boy, sitting on the bench with Hugo and the other child, presumably a friend. There was no reason why it would be here, of course – these were all photographs taken professionally, showing the splendour of the garden in its heyday, the royal visit. Two things made me shine the torch closely and bend over to peer at them. One was a photograph of Denisa Parsons. I had seen her before in the magazine Lady Alice had first shown me but here she was, I guessed, a decade older. She was a smart woman, her hair pulled back, wearing a flowered afternoon dress, earrings. Her head was thrown back and she was beaming as she pointed something out proudly to the King. I looked closely at her features. There seemed precious little resemblance between this handsome woman with the rather capacious, silk-covered bosom and the ragged, wispy-haired figure in the ancient mackintosh who had greeted me that afternoon. But faces change over the years, features decay, flesh shrivels, skin wrinkles and discolours, hair thins, teeth fall out. I could not be sure either way.

The second item was a long article from *The Times* about Denisa Parsons, the famous garden creator, internationally celebrated for what she had done at the White House. Pioneer. Plantswoman. Important Designer. Garden Visionary. The praise was effusive.

There was little about either her earlier life or her family, merely a mention of an ordinary background, marriage to Arthur Parsons, a Civil Servant in the Treasury, and two children, Margaret and Michael.

The paper was dated some thirty years ago.

I went back to my room, where the lamp had come on again. The storm was still prowling round and I could see lightning flickering across the sky occasionally as I lay in bed, sleepless.

Do I believe in ghosts? The question is common enough and, if asked, I usually hedge my bets by saying, 'Possibly.' If asked whether I have seen one, of course until now I have always said that I have not. I had not seen the ghost, for ghost it must surely be, to whom the small hand belonged, but I had felt it often enough, felt it definitely and unquestionably a number of times. I had even grown accustomed to it. Once or twice I realised that I was expecting to feel it holding my own hand. But in some strange way, the small hand was different, however ghostly it might be. Different? Different from the woman at the White House. Was she a ghost? Or had she been, as I had first assumed, a visitor, or even a squatter in the empty place, an old bag lady pretending to be Denisa Parsons? Someone who had once worked for her perhaps? The more I thought about it, the more likely that explanation seemed. It was sad to think that someone had gone back there, broken in and was living among the dirt and debris, like a rat, bundled into old clothes and spending the time looking through old scrapbooks and albums of the place in its heyday. But people do end their days in such a state, more often, I think, than we know.

It was only as I felt myself relax a little and begin to slip down into sleep that I remembered the part of the garden to which she had led me and which was tended and kept up, the grass mown, the hedges clipped, as if in preparation for opening to a party of visitors. I was confused about the place. I had walked across so many different stretches of lawn, gone through several arches cut in the yards and yards of high dark hedge, down steps, towards other enclosures, so that I had no sense of where the abandoned garden ended and the tended area began. And how many pools were there and where had the bench been on which I had apparently sat with my brother and our friend?

I drifted from remembering it all into dreaming about it, so that the real and the unreal slid together and I was walking in and out of the various parts of the garden, trying to find the right gap in the hedge, wanting to leave but endlessly sent back the way I had come, as happens to one in a maze.

I was alone, though. There was no old woman and even though at one point I seemed to have turned into myself as a boy, there were no other boys with me. Only at one point, as I tried to find my way out through yet another archway, I felt the small hand leading me on, though it felt different somehow, as befitted my dream state, an insubstantial hand which had no weight or density and which I could not grasp as I could the firm and very real flesh and bone of the hand that tucked itself into mine in my real and waking life.

Nineteen

I left for London the following morning feeling unrefreshed – I had slept, fitfully, for only a few hours and felt strung up but at least I left Sir Edgar a happy man and he had given me a new commission. He had become interested in late medieval psalters and wanted to know if I could obtain a fine example of an illuminated one. It was a tall order. Such things came on to the market very rarely, but putting out feelers, talking to people in the auction houses in both London and America, emailing colleagues, even contacting the Librarian at Saint Mathieu des Etoiles, would be very enjoyable and keep my mind away from the business at the White House. I also had some nineteenth-century salmon fishing diaries to sell for another client.

I even drove some twenty miles further, taking an indirect route back in order to avoid going anywhere near the lane leading to that place, though I knew I would not succeed in forgetting it. But I told myself sternly that speculation was fruitless.

As I neared London the traffic was heavy and I was stationary for some fifteen minutes. There was nothing remotely unusual about the place – an uninteresting stretch of suburban road. I was not thinking of the house or the garden or the hand, I was making a mental list of people I could contact with my various client requirements, remembering someone in Rome, and another in Scotland who might well be interested in the fishing books.

I glanced at the stationary traffic in the opposite lane, then in my rear-view mirror at a lorry. It did not matter that I was delayed. I had no appointment to rush to. I was simply bored.

I cannot say that anything happened. It is very difficult to explain what took place, or did not, as I waited in my car. Anyone would tell me that my imagination had been thoroughly wound up and become overexcited and likely to react to the slightest thing, because of the events of the past few weeks, and they would be right. And that is the point. My imagination did not play tricks, I heard, saw, sensed, smelled, felt nothing. Nothing. There was nothing. The strongest sensation was one of nothingness, as if I had been abandoned in some way. Nothing would come near me again, I would not be troubled or contacted. Nothing. I would never feel the sensation of the small hand in mine, or wonder if I was being watched, if something was trying to lure me into whatever lay ahead. Nothing. There was nothing. It had left me, like a fever which can suddenly, inexplicably lift, like the mist that clears within seconds.

Nothing.

I was entirely alone in my car, as the traffic began to nudge slowly forward, and I would be alone when I reached my flat. If I went back to the White House, or to the monastery, I would be alone and there would never again be a child dashing across the road through the storm in the path of my moving car.

Nothing.

I felt an extraordinary sense of release.

Half an hour later, as I walked into my flat, I knew that it had not been a fantasy, or even wishful thinking. I was free and alone, whatever it was had left me and would not return. How does one account for such strong convictions? Where had they come from and how?

Would I miss the small hand? I even wondered that for a fleeting second, because before it had begun to urge me into dangerous places, it had been strangely comforting, as if I had been singled out for a particular gentle gesture of affection from the unseen.

But the one thing I could not forget was the photograph the old woman had shown me of Hugo, his friend and me in the White House garden. I certainly had no recollection of the day or the place, but that was not surprising. I could only have been about five years old – though in the way details remain, I had remembered the Fair Isle jumper so clearly. I would ring Hugo when he was back from the States and ask him about it, though I really had no particular reason for my continuing interest except that coincidence sometimes forms a pleasing symmetry.

A COUPLE OF days later, I had a call from a dealer in New York who had a couple of items I had long been in search of and, as there were various other books I could ask about for clients while I was there, I left on a trip which then took me to San Francisco and North Carolina. I was away for three weeks, returned and flew straight off again to Munich, Berlin and then Rome and back to New York. By the time I was home, several missions having been successfully accomplished, it was late September. I was so involved with work in London for the following week or so that I completely forgot everything that had happened to me and the business of the photograph did not cross my mind.

And then I came in after dining with a potential client from Russia, to find a message from Hugo on my answerphone.

'Hi, Bro ... it's been ages ... wondered if you fancied coming up here next weekend. Benedicte's playing a concert in the church – you'd like it. Time we caught up anyway. Give us a call.'

I did so and we arranged that I would drive up to Suffolk the following Friday evening. Hugo always had an early start to his school day, so I didn't keep him long on the phone, but as we were about to ring off, I said, 'By the way ... I don't suppose you remember this any more than I do – but when we were kids, did we go with the folks to see a garden in Sussex? It was called the White House.'

I do not know what I expected Hugo to say – probably that he had no more idea than I did.

Instead, he said nothing. There was complete

silence for so long that I asked if he was still there. When he did reply, his voice sounded odd.

'Yes,' he said, 'here.'

'You don't remember anything about it, do you?'

Another silence. Then, 'Why are you asking this?'

'Oh, I just happened upon a photograph of us there – sitting on a bench outside. You, me and a friend.'

'No. There was no friend.'

'So you do remember it?'

'There was no friend. I'll see you on Friday.'

'Yes, but hang on, you …'

But Hugo had put the phone down.

Twenty

arrived in time to change quickly and go along to the church where Benedicte was playing oboe in the concert, both as orchestral member for the Bach and as soloist in the Britten *Metamorphoses*. It was a fine and rather moving occasion and neither Hugo nor I felt inclined to chat as we walked back to the house. It was a chilly night with bright stars and the faint smell of bonfires lingering on the air. Autumn was upon us.

But it was not only our rather contemplative mood after the music that prevented conversation. I could feel the tension coming from Hugo like an unspoken warning, something I had not known since the days of his illness. It was almost tangible and its message was clear – don't talk to me, don't ask questions. Back off. I was puzzled but I knew better than to try and break down the barbed-wire defences he had put up against me and we reached the house in silence.

The orchestra and performers were being given refreshments elsewhere so we had supper to ourselves, an awkward supper during which I told Hugo half-heartedly about the First Folio and something about my foreign trips, he told me tersely about Katerina's university plans and that he was wondering whether to apply for headships. If he wanted to progress up the schools career ladder, now was the time. I don't think I had ever had such a strained hour with my brother and, as we cleared up the plates, I said that I thought I would go early to bed.

But as I turned, Hugo said, 'There's something you ought to know. Have a whisky.'

We went into his study. By day this cosy room which overlooks the garden and the path to the river is flooded with light from the East Anglian sky. Now the curtains were closely drawn. Hugo switched the gas fire on, poured us drinks. Sat down. He stared into his glass, swirling the topaz liquid round, and did not speak.

I knew I should wait, not try and hurry him but

after several silent minutes I said, 'You remember all that stuff I told you … panic attacks and so forth?'

Hugo glanced at me and nodded. His expression was wary.

'You were right – they just stopped. Went. It all stopped. Whatever it was.'

'Good.'

Then I said, 'You'd better tell me.'

He swirled the whisky again, then drank it quickly.

'The other boy,' he said. 'I was there, you were there. On the bench. Then you say there was another boy? A friend, you called him. How old was he?'

I tried to bring the photograph to mind. I could see my boy-self, in the Fair Isle jumper. Hugo – I didn't remember Hugo clearly at that age, one never does, but it was Hugo.

'So far as I remember … younger than either of us, which made me wonder how he could have been a friend one of us had brought. Short hair, short grey trousers … oh, you know, like us. Just a younger boy like us.'

'What was his face like?'

I tried again but it was not clear. I had only seen the photograph once, although I had stared at it hard, in my surprise, for some moments.

I shook my head.

'There was no other boy,' Hugo said.

I opened my mouth to say that of course there was another boy, he had not seen the photograph and I had, but Hugo's face was pale and very serious.

He got up and poured us both a second whisky and, as he handed me mine, I noticed that his hand was shaking.

'The story,' he said at last, 'is this. We went twice. To that place.'

'The White House? That garden? What do you mean?'

'Mother took us. I was at prep school … at Millgate. I was out for the weekend. She brought you. It was an outing.'

I remembered little about Hugo being away at school then, though there was always a strange sense of loss, a loneliness, a hollowness at the centre of my everyday life, but by the time I was old enough to understand what it meant I had gone away to school myself, and Hugo was at Winchester.

'A boy drowned.'

I heard the words in the quiet room but it took me a moment to make sense of them.

'A boy …'

'He was the grandson – of the woman. That woman.'

'Denisa Parsons?'

'Her grandson. He was small – two? Something like that. Quite small. He drowned in the lily pond. In the garden.'

I looked at my brother. His eyes seemed to have sunken back into their sockets and his face was now deathly pale.

'How do you know this? Did someone tell you? Did mother …'

'I was there,' Hugo said. His voice was low and he seemed to be speaking half to himself. 'I was there.'

'What do you mean, "there"? At that place? Do you mean in the garden? Were we all there?'

'No. You and mother had gone to some other part – there were high hedges … arches … you'd gone through. You were somewhere else.'

He took a sip of whisky. 'I don't remember very much. I was by myself in the garden where there was – a big pool. With fish. Golden fish. Then there was – the boy. He was there. I don't remember. But he drowned. The rest is – is what we were told. Not what I remember. I remember nothing.' He looked directly across at me and his eyes seemed suddenly brilliant.

'*I remember nothing.*'

I heard Benedicte's car draw up outside and, after a moment, the front door. Hugo did not move.

'One thing,' I managed to say after a moment, 'one thing doesn't make sense. The child. The little boy fell into the pool and drowned, but what has that to do with the other boy with us in the photograph? The boy on the bench. We were both older. I don't know why she took us back – do you?'

He shrugged. 'I remember nothing.'

'Not the second visit? But you were older – what, eleven?'

'And how much do you remember of when you were eleven?'

There were footsteps across the hall and then the wireless being turned on low in the kitchen. My brother stood up.

'Hugo.'

'No,' I said. 'You started to say something, you can't leave it. You said there was no boy in the photograph. But I saw a boy. I saw him as clearly as I saw you. As I saw myself.'

He hesitated. Then waved a hand dismissively. 'Some tale,' he said. 'Always is some tale. About a boy who comes back to the garden – that boy.'

'What do ... a boy who comes back?'

'Come on. I don't believe in ghosts, nor do you.'

'Oh, as to that ... you know what happened to me. Hugo ...' I went and put my hands on his shoulders, almost shaking him in my rising anger – for it was anger, anger with him for knowing something and trying to keep it from me. 'Tell me.'

He waited until I had let my hands drop. Then he said, 'A boy – that boy I suppose. He was said to go back to the garden – ghosts do that, don't they, so the tales go? Return to the place where whatever happened – happened. He was supposed to. That's all. Just a tale.'

'But the boy who was drowned was small – two years old. This one in the photograph was older … it can't be the same. This boy in the picture was a real boy, not a ghost.'

'How do you know? How do you know what a ghost looks like? White and wispy? Half there?' He laughed, an odd little dry laugh. 'The ghost went back there every year and every year he was one year older. He was growing up – like a real boy.'

'That's not …'

'What? Not possible?'

I fell silent. None of the things that happened were possible in any normal, rational person's world. But they had happened.

'How do you know all this? You lied to me.'

'Did I?'

'When I first told you about the small hand in mine, about …'

'Oh, for God's sake, that? I shouldn't think that's got anything to do with it, should you? That was just you having a bit of a turn. Coincidence. No, no, forget about it. But if you want to know, the whole story is on the Internet. One of those spook haunting sites. I happened to be looking one night – for the boys. We'd been reading *The Turn of the Screw* … you know how it is. You start browsing around …' He laughed the short laugh again. 'Can't remember what it was called but you'll find it there. The White House ghost … all good fun.'

He drained the last of his whisky, picked up both glasses and went towards the door without saying another word. I sat on for a moment. I heard his voice, then Benedicte's, low brief snatches of talk.

I felt suddenly exhausted and my head had begun to ache. I wanted to piece together what Hugo had told me, join it up with the things that I had witnessed in the garden to make a whole picture, but they were as disconnected as jigsaw bits in my mind. I was too tired. They would come together, though, I didn't doubt it.

I might look up the story on the Internet, but something about the way my brother had talked didn't ring true. I believed he had found the story on a website, but not by accident when looking up Henry James.

THE NEXT MORNING, Hugo had gone across to school by the time I came down for breakfast, and in the afternoon he was refereeing a football match, which he did for fun, not because he was on the sports teaching team. Benedicte and I went out into the Suffolk countryside looking at churches, and ended up at a bookshop which also served teas. Over a pot, and some excellent scones, I asked her if Hugo had mentioned my brief spell of panic attacks, and whether he ever had a recurrence of them himself.

'No and no,' she said, looking surprised. 'Adam, poor you. People often laugh at such things, but they are truly awful. No, his breakdown was over and done. But I wonder, now you say this, if there was anything connecting you?'

'Runs in the family, you mean?' I shook my head. 'I doubt it. A lot of people have what I had.'

'And have you an idea why you had? Is there not always a reason?'

I hesitated, then shrugged.

She smiled. 'Well, it is all over now I hope?'

'Oh yes.'

'That's good. Because for Hugo too ... nothing ever came back. He is now very strong and sane.'

WE DROVE HOME through the darkening lanes, talking a little about music and books, more about Katerina and her prospects for getting into Cambridge to read medicine, and as we did so I felt a strange sense of lightness and well-being. The ghost story my brother had told me had explained a great deal. That the small child who had accidentally drowned should have returned to the place and wanted to be with other children seemed natural and I knew people had taken 'photographs' of ghosts. I had even seen one, a whole-school photograph with a ghostly master on the far end of the back row – though I confess I had always thought it some sort of fake. But those fakes, easy now with digital cameras, were once not so readily accomplished and as far as I could remember the boy had not looked in any way ghostly in the photograph the old woman had shown me. If he had, surely I would not just have accepted him as a third boy – our unknown 'friend'.

As I drove, I thought of the small hand, which I now believed to belong to the drowned boy. I had ventured into that place and he had caught hold of me. Had he found me every time I went near water and especially near pools? It seemed so. But why did he urge me forward? Why did I feel such fear of what might be about to happen? I shivered. It seemed beyond belief that he had such ghostly will and power that he could urge me to fall into water and drown and so join him. But what other explanation was there?

We turned into the town and drove down past the main school buildings towards the house.

Well, it was over. The ghostly power had faded. The only puzzle that remained was my visit to the White House when I had met the old woman. Had she been a ghost too? No, she had been real and substantial, though odd, but then, surviving alone in that near-derelict place would drive anyone mad. The drowned child had been her grandson and perhaps he haunted her too, perhaps she felt the small hand in hers, perhaps he took her down those gardens which led out of one another, to the place where the pool had been and that was now just a fairy ring in the ground. Poor woman. She needed help and care and company, but the world often throws up slightly deranged people like her, living on in a dream world, clinging to the past among ruins of its places. Presumably she would die there, alone, starving or ill, or in the aftermath of some accident. I wondered if I could return and talk to her again, persuade her to accept help, even to leave that dreadful, melancholy place in which her whole past life was bound up but which was not somewhere a once handsome, successful, celebrated woman should end her days. I determined to do that. And perhaps at the back of my mind was the thought that I would ask her, gently and tactfully, about her grandson, and whether the photograph was indeed of him as he might have been a few years after his death. And if she was visited by the small hand.

Even though it had left now, and I was quite free and quite unafraid, I could not yet forget the feel of it holding mine, or the effect its power had had on me.

꙳

AS WE WENT in I started to wonder if I could make the journey down to Sussex again. In any case, I expected to have news for Sir Edgar Merriman about his psalter, though I might have to take another trip to New York first. New York in the fall has a wonderful buzz, the start of the season in the auction houses, lots of new theatre, lots of good parties, the restaurants all full, but the weather still good for walking about. I felt a small dart of excitement.

AFTERWARDS, I WAS to remember that delightful sense of anticipation at the thought of New York, my last carefree, guilt-free, blithe moment. Aren't there always those moments, just before the blow falls that changes things for ever?

I went into the house behind Benedicte, who was saying that it was strange the lights were not on, that Hugo must be having a drink with the footballers, though he did not usually linger after a match. It had been a pleasant autumn day but there was a chill on the air as we had come up the path, as if there might even be a frost that night, and now I sensed that the house itself was unusually cold.

'What is …' I heard Benedicte's voice falter, as she went into the sitting room. 'Oh no … has there been a burglar in here?'

I went quickly into the room. The French windows that led to the garden were wide open. Benedicte was switching on the lamps, but as we looked round it was clear that nothing had been disturbed or, so far as we could see, taken.

'You stay here,' I said. 'I'll check.'

I went round the entire house at a run but every room was as usual, doors closed, orderly, empty.

'Adam?' Her voice sounded odd.

'Nothing and nobody there. It's all OK. Maybe you forgot to close them when we went out.'

'I didn't open them. Nobody opened them.'

'Hugo?'

'Hugo had gone to school.'

'Well, maybe he came back. Forgot his kit or – something.'

'He took his kit and why would he open these doors even if he had not?'

'He'll tell us when he gets back. I can't think of any other explanation, can you?'

There was something in her face, some look of dread or anxiety. I led her into the kitchen and opened a bottle of red wine, poured us both a large glass.

'What can I do to help with supper? Potatoes to peel, something to get from the freezer?'

Benedicte was always well organised, she would have everything planned out, even if the time we would eat was uncertain.

'Yes,' she said. I could see from her face that she was anxious. 'Some potatoes to wash and put in the oven. Baked potatoes. Sausage casserole. I thought …'

I went over to her and put my hand on her shoulder. 'You haven't been burgled,' I said. 'No one has been in here. Don't worry. Hugo will be back any minute. He can look round as well if you like. But nobody's here.'

'No,' she said.

We made preparations for supper and then took our drinks into the sitting room. I had closed and bolted the windows and drawn the heavy curtains. Benedicte switched on the gas fire. We talked a little. I read some of the paper, she went back to check the oven. Everything was as usual.

The phone rang.

‡

'Adam?'

She did not look worried then. Only puzzled.

'That was someone from school. They wanted Hugo.'

'Yes?'

'Gordon Newitt.'

I did not understand.

'The Head of Sports. He wanted Hugo. I said he was probably still having a drink with the team. But he said Hugo wasn't refereeing anything this afternoon. There was only one match and that was away. He wasn't there.'

She came further into the room and sat down suddenly. 'He wasn't refereeing any match.' She said it again in a dull voice, but her expression was still one of bewilderment, as if she were trying to make sense of what she had heard.

It may sound unbelievable to say that it was then that I knew, at that precise moment. That I knew everything, as if it had been given to me whole and entire and in every detail. I knew.

But then what I knew shattered into fragments again and I heard myself saying that the sports master had surely got it wrong, that perhaps Hugo had swapped places with someone without saying so, or that he might have gone elsewhere and confused his diary, hadn't had time to tell us, that …

I heard my own voice babbling uselessly on, saw Benedicte watching my face, as if she would read there what had really happened, where Hugo was.

And then there was a long and terrible moment of silence before I got up.

'I think I should ring the police,' I said.

Twenty-one

There is not much more of the story to tell. Hugo's body was found at first light the following morning, some way downriver. He had no injuries and the post-mortem revealed only that he had died by drowning, but not that there had been any natural reason why he should have fallen into the water – after a sudden stroke or heart attack while walking close to the edge. There was no note in the house left for his wife, no hint of any reason why he had lied about being out at the football match. We learned that he had been in school teaching on the Saturday morning, as usual and as he had said he would be. Around twelve-forty, several people had spotted him walking down the high street in the direction of home. After that, no one had seen him at all.

The towpath at that time of year is quiet but there is still the occasional dog-walker or runner. Not that afternoon.

Had he simply tripped or slipped, Benedicte asked again and again. The towpath was dry – they had had no rain for weeks, but he could have stumbled on a tree root.

It was a dreadful time. I stayed until Katerina arrived home from Cambridge and on the Monday morning I had to take Benedicte to identify Hugo's body formally.

We drove to the hospital in silence. She had been very brave and resolute, determined not to break down, and she was determined now, but she said she was afraid that she would collapse when she had to see him. That was why she wanted me with her.

I was as shocked as she was, but I had twice before had to identify bodies of the dead, including that of our father, so I did not feel any sort of fear that morning, merely a great sadness.

It was only when I looked at the still, cold body of my brother lying there that a great wave of realisation and horror broke over me. The expression on his face was blank, as it always becomes eventually, no matter what it may have been at the moment of death. It is the blank of eternal sleep.

And then I glanced at his hands. The left one was resting normally, in a relaxed position on the covering sheet. But the right one was not relaxed. Hugo's right hand was folded over, almost clenched. It looked as if it had been holding something tightly.

Of course I knew and then I understood it all, understood that the small hand which had relinquished mine for the last time had not given up, the boy had not gone away but, having failed with me, had moved to Hugo and begun to take his hand, and so draw him, clutching hard, towards the nearest water. I had not given in. I had saved myself, or been saved, though how I did not know then and I still do not know. I had not yielded to the small hand. My brother had, and died, like the boy, by drowning.

❧

I TOLD BENEDICTE none of this. We left the hospital in silence and by late that afternoon Katerina had arrived home. I left them together, partly because I felt that was what they wanted and needed but would never say, partly because I was desperate to get away. I would return for the funeral, of course, but that was not for ten days.

I drove fast away from the town and the river, desperate to put it far behind me.

I felt guilty that I had survived. I was appalled by what I knew had happened to Hugo, even though in the absence of any evidence to the contrary the coroner would record a verdict of accidental death. I would have to live with what I knew and I wondered if many others had been haunted in the same way, those who had once visited the White House garden and felt the touch of the small hand. I surely had not been the first, but I prayed that Hugo had been the last and that now the ghost of the wretched drowned boy could rest in peace.

Twenty-two

I thought that was an end to it. I thought there would be no more to tell. But there is more, another small piece of knowledge I was given and which I can never give back, can never un-know. Another, far worse thing which I must live with, for there is nothing, nothing at all, I can do with it.

When I got back home, I found a letter. It had been posted on the Saturday morning and it was addressed in my brother's hand and for a split second as I looked at the writing I forgot that he was dead but was fleetingly puzzled that he should be writing to me, on paper with pen and ink, not telephoning or sending a quick email.

But then, of course, I remembered. I realised. My

hand shook as I opened the envelope, sitting at my desk beside the window on that late afternoon of a gathering sky.

Adam,

You need to know this. I have never been able to tell you, though there have been times in these past days and weeks when I have been close to it. But in the end, I could not. Perhaps you knew I had something to say to you. Perhaps not.

Now, having decided I can live with it no longer, I must tell you.

Please remember that we were children. I was a child. At eleven years old one is still a child. I tell myself so.

The boy drowned because I pushed him into that pool. No one else was there for a moment. No one saw what happened. You came to find me and I grabbed your hand and pulled you away, up the steps and through the archway in that high hedge that has loomed so darkly through my nightmares ever since.

No one knew. It was late in the afternoon, people were leaving the gardens. We were last. I pulled you across the grass until we found Mother and then we left too.

Nothing happened for some years. I pushed it down into my unconscious, as people do with such terrible secrets. Nothing happened until my breakdown, which began suddenly and perhaps half by chance, after I read some story in the paper about a child who had drowned in a similar pool.

I had the same urges you suffered, to throw myself into water. The only difference seems to have been that I did not have to endure the grip of the small hand as you did. Not until it abandoned you – perhaps I should say 'gave up on you' – and came to me, not many weeks ago. I knew then that I should be unable to resist it, that I would have to do what it wanted, go with it. Of course I have to. It was my fault. I am guilty. You did nothing. You knew nothing.

I am sorry for this, for what I am telling you, for leaving everyone, for putting my family through what I know will be great pain. One thing, please. I beg you never to tell Benedicte or Katerina, however much you may want to unburden yourself. They will have enough to carry. Please keep this last secret between the two of us.

You are reading this in the knowledge that I have paid my debt and please God that is enough. That is an end to it all. The small ghost and I are at peace.

The last hand that other small hand will take hold of will be mine.

With my love

Hugo